She was holding her breath.

Quite why, Eloise wasn't sure. She felt herself pull her shoulders a little straighter and then heat rose to her cheeks as Celeste's nephew walked into the room.

He was blue-eyed, like Celeste. Sandy-haired, with the same-shaped face as his aunt, only the line of his jaw was a little harder and more masculine. When he smiled, there was a trace of Celeste's ebullient charm.

"It's a pleasure to meet you, Eloise." He sounded as if he actually meant it, as well. Sam Douglas advanced on her, holding out his hand.

"You, too, Sam. Welcome." Her words sounded jarringly enthusiastic. Sam was as delicious close-up as he was at a distance, perhaps more so. That was one very good reason to keep her distance, but right now it seemed there was no option but to shake his hand.

The sudden shock of his icy fingers made her jump. Or maybe it was just his touch.

Dear Reader,

There are few situations that have more potential for romance than being stranded in a beautiful historic house by a snowstorm. Venturing out into a glittering snowscape to build a snowman and then cuddling up together in front of an open fire with a glass of sparkling champagne to complete the picture…

Unfortunately, the hero and heroine of this book aren't that couple. Eloise and Sam are with their relatives, who are stranded with them. They have to work hard to help keep the local hospital running in a crisis, as well as deal with their own painful personal issues—their pasts have put them on opposing sides of similar situations!

But love can blossom in the most unlikely of places. And somehow, two cool heads and the commonplace can be turned into magic by being together.

I hope you enjoy reading Eloise and Sam's story!

Annie x

SNOWBOUND WITH HER OFF-LIMITS GP

———

ANNIE CLAYDON

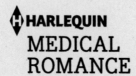

HARLEQUIN
MEDICAL
ROMANCE

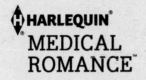

HARLEQUIN®
MEDICAL ROMANCE™

Recycling programs
for this product may
not exist in your area.

ISBN-13: 978-1-335-73749-6

Snowbound with Her Off-Limits GP

Copyright © 2022 by Annie Claydon

For questions and comments about the quality of this book, please contact us at CustomerService@Harlequin.com.

Harlequin Enterprises ULC
22 Adelaide St. West, 41st Floor
Toronto, Ontario M5H 4E3, Canada
www.Harlequin.com

Printed in U.S.A.

Cursed with a poor sense of direction and a propensity to read, **Annie Claydon** spent much of her childhood lost in books. A degree in English literature followed by a career in computing didn't lead directly to her perfect job—writing romance for Harlequin—but she has no regrets in taking the scenic route. She lives in London: a city where getting lost can be a joy.

Books by Annie Claydon

Harlequin Medical Romance

Dolphin Cove Vets
Healing the Vet's Heart

London Heroes
Second Chance with the Single Mom

Winning the Surgeon's Heart
A Rival to Steal Her Heart
The Best Man and the Bridesmaid
Greek Island Fling to Forever
Falling for the Brooding Doc
The Doctor's Reunion to Remember
Risking It All for a Second Chance
From the Night Shift to Forever
Stranded with the Island Doctor

Visit the Author Profile page
at Harlequin.com for more titles.

CHAPTER ONE

'ALL RIGHT. Out with it. What's bugging you?'

Aunt Celeste had never been slow to ask that question. Over the years, Dr Sam Douglas had replied giving details of superhero action figures that had failed to materialise when Father Christmas came to call, school exams, girlfriends and then increasingly complex medical questions. Aunt Celeste had given sage advice on them all.

'Nothing.'

'Come on, Sam. Spill.'

Sam pressed his lips together, leaning forward in the driver's seat of his car to look up at the sky. When they'd started out from London it had been a crisp and fine morning, but now that they'd reached Norfolk there were deep banks of cloud on every side of them. Now flakes of snow were beginning to drift lazily down, melting as they hit the windscreen.

'What does the weather forecast say?'

'Oh, Sam! Stop worrying about the weather, will you? If I didn't know better I'd think you were starting to sound very middle-aged...' Aunt Celeste rummaged in her handbag and Sam handed her his phone.

'It's group dynamics. You become a starry-eyed teenager and it brings out the responsible adult in me.'

Aunt Celeste laughed, tapping on the small screen in front of her. 'It says...possible snow showers tonight and tomorrow—that's all right, Paul's house looks gorgeous in the snow. Very picturesque. It snowed just before Christmas and we snuggled up together, it was wonderful.'

Perhaps Aunt Celeste hadn't yet thought of the possibility that the two dozen people who were due to arrive tomorrow evening for the weekend, to celebrate the engagement of Dr Celeste Douglas and Dr Paul Grant, might be put off by snow. Sam decided to keep his fears to himself.

'You have unread texts, darling.' Aunt Celeste's ceaseless curiosity had diverted her from any grim thoughts about the weather. 'Don't you want to stop and see who it is?'

'Not particularly. Why don't you take a look?'

Aunt Celeste gave a mock sigh. 'Since you're giving me the choice, then you clearly haven't been making very good use of your time since I saw you last. So no, you can look for yourself when we get there.'

Sam chuckled. Aunt Celeste made no secret of wanting to see him as happy as she and Paul were, but her solution was rather less open-minded than usual. Happiness consisted of finding a girlfriend who might send you the kind of texts that you didn't want your aunt to read.

He couldn't agree with her there. Happiness was being free of the way that his father had treated his mother after she'd tried to leave him. Not having to constantly examine whether his own behaviour was following the pattern of stalking and coercion that his father had established.

Alice had been the final straw, the one who had brought him to the point where being single was the only way he could find some peace. Sam had worked hard to make her as happy as he was, but Alice wanted something more. Or maybe something different. He had no way of knowing because when Alice had left she'd refused to explain why. Confusion had given way to something much darker and

Sam had made the mistake of showing his anger...

Never a good idea. Particularly when he'd seen his own father so angry with his mother on so many occasions, trying to impose his will on her. Sam had come to his senses, and not tried to contact Alice again, which was clearly exactly what she wanted because she hadn't tried to contact him.

'I think the snow's getting a little heavier.' Aunt Celeste had propped his phone back on the dashboard and was peering out of the window now.

'We'll make it. Even if I have to carry you through a blizzard.'

Aunt Celeste reacted just as he'd wanted to the hyperbole and let out an amused *Ha!* 'I appreciate the thought, but that's not going to be necessary—we'll be there in less than half an hour. Anyway, Paul and I have waited long enough for this and I'll have you know that if there's any carrying to be done you'll be stepping aside and allowing him to do it.'

Paul Grant was the spryest seventy-year-old that Sam had ever met, in addition to being a very eminent paediatrician. And he and Aunt Celeste were good together.

Sam smiled. 'Nothing can come between you, eh?'

'As it happens, no. Despite our advanced age.' Aunt Celeste shot him a defiant look.

'Hey, you don't need to convince me, you know that. What didn't you understand about my saying I was thrilled for you both?'

'Thank you, darling. There have been a few whispers.'

About a Douglas marrying a Grant? Sam had shrugged that one off as being ridiculous. And so what if Celeste Douglas was sixty-five and Paul Grant was seventy? Love was hard to find, and even harder to keep, Alice had shown him that. Paul and Aunt Celeste had managed to beat all of the odds and take a fragile and elusive thing and turn it into gold. That should never be dismissed.

'Whispering because they didn't dare make such a ridiculous suggestion out loud?'

Aunt Celeste chuckled. 'Point taken. And if the snow gets worse and no one turns up we're not going to let it cramp our style, are we?'

Sam was happy with that. A few days spent with two of his favourite people, without being faced with questions about how his mother was doing, as if she'd been frozen in time and after twenty years was still a victim. None of the polite avoidance of any mention of his father, or the way he'd died either.

Aunt Celeste frowned suddenly, as if she'd just thought of something. 'Although Paul mentioned last night that he'd asked his granddaughter to come down early and help with all the preparations…'

'Then I won't be playing gooseberry, will I? Is this the granddaughter that's a doctor?' Sam grinned at his aunt. Just as most of the Douglas family were doctors, so were most of the Grants.

'That's a very safe guess, on the basis that three out of four of them are and the one who isn't is in Australia at the moment.'

'Then we'll have something to talk about, while you and Paul exercise your ingenuity over finding quiet corners to canoodle in.'

That brought a smile to Aunt Celeste's lips. 'Ingenuity is always worth the effort, I find. And Eloise is a very nice girl, whatever anyone says.'

Eloise Grant. Sam had heard Aunt Celeste mention the name before, but he couldn't place her.

'You know I don't have much truck with gossip.'

'If the Grants don't turn up you won't be bothered with it. But if they do manage to brave the weather…' Aunt Celeste pressed her lips together. 'I can't tell you the exact truth of it, because I don't know either. Eloise told Paul, but he hasn't told me. I respect that in him, that he can keep a confidence.'

Sam chuckled. 'That's got to be driving you crazy.' Aunt Celeste's curiosity and her belief that talking about things was always a positive step were no great secret.

'I understand completely. She needs to talk about it in her own time, and I don't see why anyone thinks that she has to justify her actions to them. It's a matter of principle.' Aunt Celeste grimaced. 'Yes, it's driving me crazy.'

That was that, then. Sam was more than happy to just follow instructions and close his ears to anything that resembled gossip, but it was no surprise that Aunt Celeste wasn't content to leave the matter there.

'Eloise was involved in a scandal a year ago. We all turned up to her wedding and her fiancé was left standing at the altar. He seemed quite heartbroken. His mother said that they'd all had an inkling that something was wrong, but that this had come as a complete surprise. Although quite what he was doing standing in the church looking surprised if he *did* know that something was wrong…'

People didn't always act logically. Breaking off a relationship was never easy, and

Sam had made it harder for Alice by believing that they could work things out and becoming increasingly angry when she refused to give him any chance of doing so. It was possible that Eloise Grant understood why a woman might refuse point-blank to explain, the way that Alice had done, but the trickle of alarm that was currently working its way down Sam's spine told him that he was better off not knowing.

'She just disappeared, for two weeks. Then she *had* to come back because of her job, but she's only ever spoken to Paul about why she did it. I've always rather felt that she was misjudged over that.'

Sam tried to shake off the conflicting feelings of *having* to know why but not wanting to. He'd told everyone that he and Alice had parted amicably and it had been a joint decision. Aunt Celeste wasn't tactless, and she probably wouldn't be saying all of this now if she knew that Sam was still quietly agonising over reasons that Alice shouldn't have had to give but his raging heart had demanded of her.

'Misjudged, how?' He didn't want to ask, but not asking was unbearable.

'Since Eloise wasn't there to give her side of things, the Grants all immediately believed the fiancé and thought that Eloise had acted very badly. I didn't like him all that much. He was much too charming...'

'You don't like charming?' Sam was running on automatic now, keeping his eyes fixed on the road.

Aunt Celeste gave the same *Don't-you-know-anything?* sigh that had punctuated his teens. 'I like thoughtfulness and sincerity in a man. I'd describe that as charming. I don't have much time for charming as a means to an end.'

It was just like Aunt Celeste to pick a different side from the one everyone expected her to. She was his father's sister, but even at the height of the battle between his parents she'd kept an open mind. She'd supported his mother, along with Sam and his brother and sister, at the same time making it clear that she was able to still love his father even if she didn't approve of his actions. When the restraining order had finally persuaded his father that the marriage was over, and he'd started to drink heavily, it had been Aunt Celeste who had moved heaven and earth, trying to get him some help.

'And what's your means to an end in telling me all this?'

'Am I really *that* transparent?'

Sam flashed her a smile. 'Always. It's one of the things I like about you.'

'You're a kind man, Sam. Paul was worried that Eloise would find some excuse not to make this weekend, because of all the gossip. She's been… I would say hurt, but I get the feeling it's more a case of having been damaged. After everything you went through in your teens, with your father, you know how that feels, don't you?'

He did, but that didn't mean he knew what to do about it. Aunt Celeste could be a little too confident in people sometimes, and the idea of following Eloise if she ran from a crowd of disapproving relatives, and making everything right for her, seemed impossible. Even if he had the heart for it, and right now he wasn't sure whether simply passing the time of day might not be too challenging.

And then, unexpected as always, Aunt Celeste saved him from the awkwardness of a conversation that he'd really rather not be having.

'Sam! You missed the turning!'

'Uh? Oh… Yeah.' In his determination to focus on the road ahead and not Eloise Grant, he'd driven straight past the wrought iron gates that accessed the tree-lined drive that led to Paul's house. Sam slowed the car, turning around.

When he drew up outside the magnificent Tudor manor house he stayed in his seat for a moment, wondering what the next few days might bring. Aunt Celeste turned her astute blue-eyed gaze onto him.

'Are you all right, darling?'

'Why wouldn't I be?' Sam decided to forget about everything else and concentrate on the next few moments. 'I thought you might want me to stay out of the way while you raced to the front door and melted into your fiancé's arms.'

Aunt Celeste rolled her eyes. 'Practicality before romance, Sam. Slipping on a patch of ice and falling flat on your face isn't a good look, at any age. I thought we'd decided that *you* were going to be the adult of the two of us…'

Eloise's grandfather was standing at the window of the large sitting room, made cosy by a roaring fire. His hands were in his pockets and he was looking silently out at the flurries of snow.

Eloise knew why she was here, earlier than all the rest of the guests, and in possession of one of the sprawling old manor house's seven bedrooms, instead of staying at a nearby hotel like most of the other guests. It was Gramps' way of telling the rest of the family that he supported her and that anyone who didn't shouldn't bother to attend the party. It crossed Eloise's mind that Gramps' gesture had back-fired pretty spectacularly and that her mere presence was about to jinx the whole weekend.

'I'm sorry, Gramps.' Eloise joined him at the window.

'What have you done now? Broken all the best china?' Gramps smiled mischievously down at her.

'I'm sorry that it's snowing.'

'Ah. Someone's put you in charge of the weather?'

It was difficult to resist Gramps. Eloise nudged his elbow with hers. 'Perhaps I should rephrase. I'm sorry to see that it's snowing.'

'Better.'

Gramps had been a tower of strength. He was the closest family member she had left, and when she'd returned from the hotel she'd been hiding out in after her wedding was cancelled, Eloise had come here. He'd asked no questions, simply hugging her and being there for her when the whole story had come spilling out.

The stream of condemnation from her family had been partly her fault, because she could have managed things a great deal better. The day before the wedding had been a nightmare of discovery and confrontation, and she'd suddenly seen Michael in a completely different light. When Eloise had asked him if it was true that he'd fathered a child with his previous partner, and had rejected every opportunity to see the boy, he hadn't denied it.

The promise of spending her life with the man she loved, and who she could trust to do the right thing, had been ripped in two, but she'd tried to salvage it and told Michael she'd support him in forming a relationship with his son. He'd been angry, raging at her that if she was going to spoil all of his plans for their future together by dwelling on a minor inconvenience from his past then the wedding was off. They'd managed to stay civil with each other long enough to compose an email to send to all of the guests, and then Michael's face had hardened again and he'd told her to leave everything to him and get out of his sight.

She'd trusted Michael one last time and left, running away from the dream that had come crashing down. It was only when she'd returned that she'd realised that the email had never been sent, and that Michael had diverted any awkward questions about his own part in the sudden separation by pretending she'd unexpectedly left him at the altar. In her absence there had been ample time for the gossip to turn her into a monster.

Her extended family might have trusted her enough to wait and listen to her side of the story, but they hadn't. Eloise had been met by minds that were already made up, and everyone had expected her to apologise for leaving Michael. When she'd refused there was little more to be said. So it had become increasingly easy to apologise for everything else, snow included.

Gramps was craning forward, trying to see as far along the drive as possible.

Eloise nudged him again. 'Celeste is on her way. She'll be here soon.'

Gramps chuckled. 'I know. Give me the pleasure of waiting impatiently for her, eh? Even if you're not quite sure I'm doing the right thing.'

'She makes you happy. What's not to like about that?' Eloise *wasn't* sure. She liked and respected Celeste, but still couldn't quite chase away the feeling that any relationship carried with it the risk of heartbreak. Gramps was semi-retired now, and he deserved to look forward with some guarantee of peace.

'I'm curious. Do you honestly think that Celeste has it in her to keep secrets from me? Even if she really set her mind to it…' Gramps smirked down at her. 'I couldn't keep anything from her either.'

'Apart from *my* secrets.' Eloise wondered if she hadn't asked a bit too much of Gramps, but he'd volunteered the suggestion that he'd say nothing to anyone.

'That's different, and Celeste understands that. She believes in talking about things, but she also believes that you should do it in your own time, and not give in to other people pressuring you. As do I.'

Eloise gave Gramps a hug. 'What would I do without you both?'

Gramps smiled. 'Not everyone's like Michael, you know. One day you'll get around to trusting in that belief.'

One day. Not today, though.

'Let's just concentrate on you and Celeste until that happens, shall we?'

Eloise couldn't spoil this moment for him. As a dark blue SUV drove slowly into the courtyard in front of the house she saw Gramps smile with excitement.

The occupants of the car seemed to be talking for a moment. Then a man got out of the driver's seat, pulling on a thick fur-collared parka that made his shoulders seem even broader and making his way round to the passenger door to offer Celeste his arm as she emerged from the car. Gramps only had eyes for her as she took a few steps and then seemed to change her mind, letting go of the man's arm and waving him away, before heading for the door at a faster pace.

Gramps hurried to open the door for her. Something made Eloise stay at the window. Maybe the notion that Gramps and Celeste would want a few moments alone to greet each other. Maybe she just couldn't take her eyes off the man as he watched Celeste, an amused look on his face, and then made his way back to the car to fetch the suitcases.

This must be Celeste's nephew. Gramps had told her about Dr Sam Douglas, and how close he and Celeste were, but the first thing about him that Eloise noticed was that he had the most gorgeous smile. A shiver ran down her spine as she watched him heave the suitcases effortlessly from the boot of the car.

She was out of the habit of appreciating a stranger's smile. That wasn't altogether a bad thing, since the charm and the smile of the man she'd once loved had made it so very difficult for her to see the truth about him.

'Darling…!' Celeste appeared in the doorway. 'We made it! Although it looks as if the weather's taking a turn for the worse.'

'I'm sure it'll clear up soon.' Eloise glanced back at the window in the hope of seeing some evidence of that, but the snow showed no signs of stopping. But Celeste looked so excited and Gramps was smiling so broadly that now wasn't the time to wonder whether the guests who were expected tomorrow would be able to make it.

Celeste flapped her hand cheerfully. 'It doesn't matter. The four most important people are already here, and we won't be able to help having a wonderful time, will we Paul?'

'I can't see how we can manage to avoid it.' Gramps was smiling and Eloise couldn't resist following suit. It was nice to be called an important person in an engagement celebration, instead of being consigned to a corner as if she'd put a hex on the marriage just by being there.

'Sam…' Celeste called out into the corridor as the front door slammed shut. 'Come and meet Eloise…'

She was holding her breath. Quite why, Eloise wasn't sure. She felt herself pull her shoulders a little straighter and then heat rose to her cheeks as Celeste's nephew walked into the room.

He was blue-eyed, like Celeste. Sandy-haired, with the same face shape as his aunt, only the line of his jaw was harder and more masculine. When he smiled, there was a trace of Celeste's ebullient warmth.

'It's a pleasure to meet you, Eloise.' He sounded as if he actually meant it as well. Sam Douglas advanced on her, holding out his hand.

'You too, Sam. Welcome.' Her words sounded jarringly enthusiastic. Sam was as delicious close-up as he was at a distance, perhaps even more so. That was one very good reason to keep her distance, but right now it seemed there was no option but to shake his hand.

The sudden shock of his icy fingers made her jump. Or maybe it was just his touch. Sam grinned suddenly, making Eloise feel even more awkward.

'Sorry. Cold hands.' He took a step back, holding his hands out to the roaring fire in the grate.

'Quite unforgivable in a GP,' Celeste teased him. 'Eloise works in Accident and Emergency.'

Sam turned, giving Eloise another spine-tingling smile. 'Only in this family, eh? We've barely been introduced, and we already know what kind of doctors we are.'

Actually that was something of a relief. Eloise would far rather be judged as a doctor than anything else, because in that sphere at least it was considered that she had something to give. She was actually beginning to wish that the snow would get a little heavier because, even if Celeste didn't know all the details, she'd always dismissed the gossip as hurtful rubbish. And the look in Sam's eyes gave no hint that he knew anything about it. Eloise felt a sudden swell of warmth towards them both.

'You must be famished. I have soup and sandwiches waiting for you in the kitchen.'

Concentrating on food, in the cool air of the kitchen, might dispel some of the heat that seemed to be radiating from her, quell the irrepressible thought that Sam could warm his hands against her skin any time he liked.

Celeste took off her coat, displaying a thick purple sweater with an iridescent scarf. 'Wonderful! I'll come and help.'

'No you don't. Stay here and warm up by the fire.' She hadn't been able to help noticing Sam's scent, and she needed some time alone to talk some sense into herself. Eloise didn't wait for anyone to protest, leaving Gramps to sort out the coats and hurrying to the kitchen.

CHAPTER TWO

THE WOMAN WHO had left a relationship without feeling the need to explain why. As soon as Sam had laid eyes on her, he forgot all about how much he'd been hurt when Alice had done the same to him.

It was tempting to feel that someone so luminously beautiful couldn't be all bad. Sam knew that looks were never a measure of character. But someone that vulnerable? He might not be able to put his finger on any one thing that she did which made him come to that conclusion, but vulnerability was one of those things that people wore. Like happiness or grief, or any of the other feelings that seemed to soak through a person and shape them.

And he couldn't deny that she *was* beautiful. Her thick sweater and jeans couldn't disguise a light grace of movement. Dark hair, piled up on the back of her head so that it revealed the fine curve of her neck. Dark eyes, whose depths seemed to contain every thought, every possibility, that the world around her could offer.

Aunt Celeste and Paul were sitting on the sofa together, talking happily, and Sam chose one of the armchairs by the fire. Eloise returned with a tray, refusing to let anyone get up and help her with the rest of the lunch things. And when she finally did sink into an armchair she seemed on the alert still, relaxing only when Aunt Celeste pronounced that everything was quite delicious and absolutely perfect.

A people pleaser, then. Sam seemed to be turning into an amateur detective, assessing the lines of tension on her brow and the way her gaze darted from one person to another, checking that everyone was in agreement with Aunt Celeste's opinion. The dark shadows under her eyes might give some clue to a sleepless night, over something that was worrying her...

And on the other hand they might be the result of something completely different. Amateur psychologist took over from amateur detective and started making a similar list of unqualified pronouncements. Maybe his fascination with her was something to do with a yearning to repeat past experiences, in the hope that they might work out better than they had with Alice…

Paul's phone rang, and Celeste fell silent suddenly. A quick conversation, that everyone got the gist of, and then he ended the call.

'That was my sister…' Paul turned his lips down as he addressed Celeste. 'She wants to know what the weather's going to be like tomorrow.'

'Oh, really…' Aunt Celeste laughed. 'As if any of us knows that. I'm glad you told her to go with the flow. I'm sure everything will work out one way or another.'

Eloise frowned, picking up her phone. Pretty much a perfect frown, indicating that something was amiss but she was about to correct it. Sam wondered whether she considered herself responsible for the weather, and toyed with a vision of her banishing the clouds and summoning sunshine.

'They say that we can expect more tomorrow…' Her frown deepened, as if she was working on that.

'There's your chance, darling!' Paul flashed a mock-serious look at Aunt Celeste. 'If marrying someone who lives in the path of a cold northerly airstream is going to be a problem you'd better say so now, before it's too late.'

'I'm thinking about it.' Aunt Celeste was smiling up at him, clearly not thinking about it at all.

It didn't take a detective or a psychologist to work out that they were joking, but the look of sudden uncertainty on Eloise's face betrayed a flash of doubt. Sam laughed quietly, wondering if that might prompt Aunt Celeste to make the inevitable choice a bit more quickly.

It didn't. Aunt Celeste and Paul were still teasing each other, each of them playing hard to get. But suddenly Sam found himself drowning, lost in Eloise's gaze, and the way that she suddenly smiled in response to his prompt. Breathless, he was pulled inexorably down by the feeling that making her smile was the one and only thing he wanted to do. Feeling his fingertips tingle as his heart pumped out the message that her smile was so easily won, and then wondering what on earth had happened to make her so fearful for Paul and Aunt Celeste.

She gave a little shake of her head and then a shrug, as if to acknowledge her mistake. For a moment there was more, as if she saw everything about him even though they'd only just met. And then suddenly she got to her feet, catching up a folded piece of paper from behind a glass ornament on the deep stone hearth.

'Do you think we should call everyone? Let them know to keep an eye on the weather forecast for Norfolk?'

She held the sheet out to Paul, clearly hesitant to do it herself, and he nodded, taking it. 'Yes, I think that's a good idea, Eloise.'

Paul had started to make the calls, Aunt Celeste sitting beside him, adding her good wishes to his when he finished each one. Eloise had made coffee and then returned to sit on the other side of him and check the list of guests as he worked through it. Sam drank his coffee, then took the suitcases upstairs, finding that each bedroom had a name card affixed to the door. Paul's had pink hearts drawn around his and Aunt Celeste's names, and when he opened the door to put her case inside he smelled flowers and saw a bright arrangement on a sturdy chest of drawers by the window, along with a glass bowl which, if he wasn't much mistaken, contained Aunt Celeste's favourite chocolates.

Sam walked to the end of the hallway, past the bedrooms labelled *Grant*, and found *Sam Douglas*, unable to stop himself from pausing for a moment to look at the careful penmanship. Inside, the room was warm and inviting. The grand old fireplace, the wood panelling and the windows that stretched around two sides of the room were fixtures, but the arrangement of red-berried holly on the mantelpiece and the towels carefully folded on the bed were finishing touches that didn't seem much like Paul and Aunt Celeste's jolly *make-yourself-at-home* attitude. The last time he'd been here he'd been told where his bed was, given permission to take whatever he wanted from the fridge and left to his own devices.

Maybe Eloise felt she had something to prove. When he opened the door of the bulky old armoire the smell of sandalwood drifted out and he saw fresh lining paper on the shelves. It seemed that Eloise felt she had more than just something to prove...

Sam unpacked his case, reckoning that the phone calls might take a while. It was still snowing outside, making the warmth of the room seem even more cosy, and he resisted the temptation to stay here and read the book he'd brought with him. He should brave the terrors of the sitting room, and the ultimate discomfort of finding that the woman who he'd rashly assumed might be someone he wanted to avoid had caught his attention and wasn't letting go.

When he returned to the sitting room, Aunt Celeste informed him that everyone had been contacted and some had already expressed doubts about whether they'd make it tomorrow. They were, however, going to make the best of things. Paul laughingly agreed and that was that.

'I have to go down to the village.' Eloise smiled, tapping the side of her nose when Paul shot her an enquiring look. 'Just errands.'

'Can it wait?' Paul asked.

'I may as well go now; it doesn't look as if it's going to stop snowing.'

'I'll come with you, then....' Paul stood and Aunt Celeste got from her seat as well. Eloise was shaking her head, telling them to stay by the fireside together, and they were protesting that they wouldn't let her go alone, and then Sam heard his own voice, coming from a place that seemed unfamiliar to him.

'I'll go with Eloise. You two stay here.'

Everyone looked at him. It made perfect sense. Paul and Aunt Celeste could stay here, whispering a few sweet nothings to each other, and instead of uneasily playing gooseberry Sam would go with Eloise. The other voice in his head, warning him to stay away from Eloise, was quiet for a moment, as if it knew that a ten-minute walk down to the village couldn't possibly do any harm, and it was the obvious thing to do in the circumstances.

'I can pick up anything you need.' Eloise was looking at him uncertainly, although Paul and Aunt Celeste seemed happy with the arrangement.

Then Sam's instinct kicked in. She was vulnerable, eager to please, and the thought that he needed to stay away from her seemed suddenly ridiculous. He summoned up his easiest smile.

'I could do with stretching my legs…'

Suddenly, she was the only person in the room. And when she smiled, that was the only thing that mattered to him.

'Okay I'll get my coat.'

Eloise was wearing a dark blue parka and a bright red knitted hat pulled down over her ears, which made her delicate features seem even more charming and elf-like. Large flakes of snow were drifting lazily down now, and enough had settled to leave two sets of footprints behind them on the drive, Eloise's smaller ones next to his.

They'd been walking silently, and Sam turned to look back at the house. The redbrick arches above the doors and windows were lined with snow, and the roof was al-most covered.

'It looks very picturesque in the snow, doesn't it?' He heard Eloise's voice beside him. 'If things just stay like this it'll be per-fect. Enough snow to make the place look magical, and not enough to stop people from getting here.'

That was a big ask. In Sam's experience the weather was usually too much of some-thing or not enough of it, but Eloise seemed so determined that this weekend should be just right.

'Paul and Aunt Celeste appear to think that everything already is perfect...' Love—true love—was almost impossibly hard to find, but if you did it was resilient and couldn't be ruined by everyday difficulties.

From her expression, Eloise clearly didn't quite agree with that. But she said nothing, turning to make her way around the curve of the driveway to the high wall that surrounded the property.

Outside, there seemed to be more people walking than driving, just a few sets of tyre marks on the road and many footprints on the path that ran alongside it. Sensible, since conditions weren't great for driving and ice was forming in the indentations of tyre tracks.

Someone had obviously already skidded to one side...

Just as Sam realised that there were no tracks that indicated the mystery car had corrected its course, he saw Eloise quicken her pace. Up ahead, there was a gap in the sparse hedge that lined the other side of the road.

She was running now and he followed, struggling to keep up with her on the slippery surface. When he got to the hedge he saw a small SUV, nose down at the bottom of a shallow embankment on the other side, and Eloise slithering down towards it.

Sam followed, and by the time he reached the car, Eloise had already carefully opened the driver's door. He could see a woman in the back seat, a boy of around five in her lap, and a baby carrier that was covered with a blanket next to her.

'Bess...' Eloise clearly knew her. 'Are you hurt?'

The woman seemed uninjured and had started to cry with relief. 'No, we're okay. We weren't going at any speed, and the car just slid off the road. Thank goodness you're here, Eloise...' Bess shifted the boy from her lap, starting to clamber forward between the seats.

'Sit tight for a minute. I'm going to get in

and just check on you and the kids...' Eloise reached in, laying her hand on Bess's shoulder in a reassuring gesture.

'No! Eloise, you don't understand. It's Gran. She's fallen and she's out in the cold...'

Eloise's face set in an expression of determination. 'Where is she? At home?'

Bess nodded miserably. 'In the back garden. She's got one of those alarm buttons where you can talk to the operator, and they called me. They've called an ambulance as well, but I thought I could get to her more quickly.'

'Okay. One minute.' She turned to Sam. 'If I go back and get my car, can you stay with Bess?'

Not a trace of *If-that's-okay-with-you?* or *If-you-don't-mind?* in her expression. She'd already made her decision about the best way to do this and Sam nodded in agreement.

'Take mine if you want—the key's on the hall table.' His four-wheel drive would probably handle the conditions better than the blue run-around he'd parked next to this morning.

Eloise gave him a smiling nod, turning quickly back to Bess. 'Give me the keys, Bess, and I'll go over there now. Sam's a doctor, he'll stay with you.'

Bess seemed about to protest, and then

thought better of it. Eloise's tone brooked no argument, and as soon as Bess had handed over a keyring with two keys on it from her handbag she started to scramble back up the embankment. Something told Sam that there was no need to turn and watch her go, because Eloise wouldn't look back for the reassurance she'd seemed to crave earlier on.

He took her place at the door of the vehicle, leaning in. Bess had dissolved into tears now, but he needed her to keep her cool for a little while longer.

'Bess… I'm Sam. Look at me. How long have you been here?'

'Not long… Ten minutes maybe… I called Tom, my husband, but he's at work and it'll take him another half an hour to get here. I didn't dare leave the car, because I wasn't sure I could get up the embankment with both of the kids…' Bess was getting more and more agitated.

'That's okay, Bess. You've done really well, and I want you to take a couple of slow breaths for me.' Sam waited while she did so. 'You're sure that neither you or the children are hurt?'

'No, we're okay. They were both strapped into their seats, and Aaron's been talking to me.' Bess drew the little boy back onto her lap.

Sam reached forward, moving the blanket that covered the baby carrier so that he could see inside. The baby seemed warm and responsive and when Sam turned his attention to Aaron the little boy stuck his tongue out cheekily.

'Please, Sam. I'm so worried about my grandmother...'

Sam didn't envy Bess's situation—torn between keeping her children safe and the knowledge that her grandmother urgently needed help.

His priorities were clear though; Eloise's decision had made that possible. His first concern was Bess and the children, while hers was Bess's grandmother.

'Eloise is on her way to your grandmother, Bess. I'm here for you. We're going to take the children up to Paul Grant's house.'

Bess nodded, opening the back door of the car so that Sam could unclip the baby carrier. She and Aaron climbed forward and got out of the car, and Sam motioned to her to start walking with the boy, the few hundred yards to where the embankment was less steep.

He'd caught up with her by the time they reached the hedge. Sam pushed through, holding the baby carrier out of reach of the bare frozen twigs, catching little Aaron when he evaded his mother's grasp and scrambled through on his own. He could see part way along the drive that led to the manor house now and Paul and Aunt Celeste were hurrying towards them, zipping up their coats as they came.

Bess pushed through the hedge and as he shepherded the family across the road he saw his own car, the windscreen hastily cleared, nosing its way towards them. Sam gave the baby carrier to Aunt Celeste and set Aaron back onto his feet so that Paul could take his hand. His car drew up beside them, and the passenger door was pushed open.

'Get in…'

Sam hesitated for a brief moment, wondering whether Eloise was going to slide out of the driver's seat. Apparently not.

'I know the way. And I'm a very good driver.'

He couldn't help a smile as he got into his car. He'd just met a different Eloise, decisive and suddenly confident, and he already liked this side of her much better than the one he'd been introduced to.

The thought of Granny June outside in the snow had pushed Eloise forward, across the slippery ground and back to the house. Calling to Gramps and Celeste while she found the keys to Sam's car, she'd left them to hurry down to meet Bess, while she quickly grabbed the medical kit that Gramps kept ready in the cupboard under the stairs. She'd hurriedly cleared the windscreen of the worst of the snow and ice and started the car, going as fast as she dared on the driveway.

At the back of her mind, she was wondering if Sam had got Bess and the children out of the car yet. She might need some help when she got to Granny June's, particularly if the ambulance hadn't arrived. The relief when she saw him crossing the road wasn't entirely in response to that.

Tall and broad, holding the baby carrier in one hand, his other arm supporting Aaron against his chest. The little boy's arms were flung around his neck and Bess was walking beside him, her smaller frame shivering in the icy wind.

It was a brief snapshot, but it embodied all you would want in a man. Strong and yet caring. Good with kids—Michael's behaviour had made that one particularly important. Brave and resourceful couldn't really be applied to pushing your way through a hedge that wasn't thick enough to put up much resistance, but Eloise's imagination was on a roll…

The windscreen was starting to mist, and when Sam got into the car he pressed the controls to open the windows of both the driver's and front passenger's doors. Her view of the road ahead cleared suddenly and the blast of cold air had the added advantage of bringing her to her senses. She'd accepted Michael as her own personal hero far too readily, and making that mistake again would be reckless.

'How far is it?' Sam had been sitting quietly in the passenger seat, but clearly he was as eager to get to Granny June as she was.

'It's not far, she lives in Mazingford.' Eloise turned off the road into the minor road that was signposted to Mazingford, feeling the car begin to slip slightly on the icy road. He must feel it too and she wondered if he was beginning to regret letting her drive.

'I've got it…' She changed gear and felt the tyres grip again.

'I know.'

She didn't have time to debate whether this was wishful thinking on Sam's part, or he really was that confident in her. Mazingford High Street was up ahead, and Granny June's cottage was in one of the small roads on the left. She drew up outside Granny June's yellow front door, turning to reach for Gramps' medical bag on the back seat.

Sam turned too, smiling when he saw the bag. 'I'll bring this. Go and get the front door open...'

Eloise jogged to the door, her hands shaking as she put the key into the lock. She had to forget everything else now. All the times she and Bess had played at Granny June's when she was little, and spent her summers here with Gramps. Everything that had happened since, and the feeling that she had somehow to prove to Sam that the gossips were wrong about her. None of that mattered right now. What mattered was that she had a patient who was in need of her professionalism.

She ran through the house, opening the back door. At the end of the path, next to the bird table, she could see Granny June, lying motionless in the snow. As Eloise started forward, her heart thumping with trepidation, Granny June moved. She stumbled towards her, kneeling down in the snow.

'Eloise...' Granny June trembled out her name.

'Hey there, Granny June. Bess sent me.'

Granny June was well wrapped up, in a long waterproof parka and fur-lined boots, and it seemed that they had done their job in keeping her relatively dry. Curling her hand carefully behind Granny June's head, to protect it from the cold ground, Eloise started to tick off the points on her mental checklist.

Then the crunch of footsteps behind her and the sound of the heavy medical kit being put down onto the ground told her that Sam was there.

'I don't see any blood. She's breathing without difficulty and...' Her fingers found Granny June's pulse. 'Sixty BPM...'

'Not bad, eh?' Granny June's voice was weak but she was alert and coherent.

'I'd put it at very good.' She heard Sam's voice behind her. 'You'll be inside in the warm very soon, but bear with me while I do a few very quick checks to make sure you didn't hurt yourself when you fell.'

Eloise turned, giving him a quick nod. There was a reason why you didn't assess and treat friends and family for traumatic injury unless it was unavoidable. Sam could take that step back and make cool-headed decisions about Granny June's medical condition. The risk of moving her had to be weighed carefully against the obvious need to get her inside and out of the cold, and now wasn't the time for Eloise to be showing him how well she could handle a situation.

A woman's voice crackled through the alarm that Granny June had around her neck.

'Are you still there, my love? What's happening?'

'I'm here…' Granny June's voice seemed a little stronger now.

'I'm here too, I'm a doctor. My colleague is examining June and we'll have her inside in the warm as quickly as we can.' Eloise bent over, speaking into the small intercom.

'Thank goodness. Is there anything I can do for you? Call someone?'

Eloise thought quickly. Bess was waiting for news, and Gramps could be trusted to give that news to her reassuringly, without making any rash promises. She gave his phone number to the woman, who read it back carefully.

'You'll be speaking with Dr Paul Grant, he's with June's granddaughter now. Please tell him that we're here, and checking June over for injuries, but she seems okay…'

'I'm fine!' Granny June interrupted. 'I just wish I could get up!'

Eloise heard the woman laugh, and then her voice became businesslike again. 'Got it. I'll call him right now. And you are?'

'Dr Eloise Grant. Tell him we'll be moving June into the warm as soon as possible.'

'I could really do with a cup of tea!' Granny June shot Eloise a reproachful look.

'I'll bet you could,' the woman replied. 'I'm

going to leave you now that you're safe. Good luck…'

'Thank you, dear.'

Before Eloise could add her own thanks, there was a click as the operator closed the connection to the intercom. Eloise made a silent promise to herself to find the woman and thank her for everything she'd done, and set about checking Granny June's hands for injury. They were so cold, and all she wanted to do was hug her.

'Any pain?' She heard Sam's voice behind her.

'I don't think so. Granny June, do you feel any pain? Don't be brave now, you must tell me.'

'No pain.'

'Did you hit your head when you fell?'

'No, darling. I just…slid. But I couldn't get up again.'

Sam would be checking for a broken hip, to see if that had caused the fall. It would be obvious and something they needed to take heed of when moving her. He was working quickly, covering all of the bases, but Granny June's face registered no pain.

'No blood or bumps at the back of her head?' Sam murmured the question quietly.

'No…not as far as I can tell.'

'Right then. Time to get you inside for that cup of tea.' Sam gave Granny June the most reassuring smile that Eloise had ever seen.

Granny June smiled back, trusting him. Eloise might have a better appreciation than she did of all the things that might go wrong, but somehow that smile seemed to work into her soul, demanding that she should be confident.

Sam waited for her to position herself so that they could lift Granny June together, one on each side of her. Then, on his word, they carefully guided her to her feet.

'Try just one step for me, June.' He was smiling still, watching carefully as Granny June slowly took a step, wincing as she did so.

'My ankle hurts a bit.'

'Okay, don't put any weight on it. Eloise and I will support you. Anything else? Your back or your hips?'

Granny June shook her head. Carefully, slowly they made their way to the back door, and Sam reached forward to open it. The kitchen/diner was warm and cosy after the chill of the garden, and Granny June was led to the banquette that stood at the far end of the dining table, giving a deep sigh as she was carefully lowered onto it.

'Better now?' Sam asked and Granny June

nodded. 'We'll just get your coat and boots off, shall we? That'll help you warm up a bit.'

Eloise fetched a footstool from the front parlour and Sam lifted Granny June's feet onto it, taking off her boots and carefully inspecting her ankle. He pronounced it a little swollen and said that it should be checked over at the hospital, and left Eloise with Granny June while he put the kettle on for a cup of tea.

'My fingers hurt.' June looked at her bright red hands with dismay.

'That's because they're warming up. We'd be more worried if you couldn't feel them.'

June regarded her thoughtfully. 'Is Sam your friend, dear?'

Granny June was clearly feeling much better now, and the question wasn't as innocent as it sounded. She was always on the lookout for good boyfriend material for Eloise, and Sam was admittedly *very* good boyfriend material. Good lover material as well, if she wasn't very much mistaken.

'No, he's Celeste's nephew.'

'Ah. Nice.' Granny June was looking at Sam speculatively as he made the tea, clearly not ready to give up on his potential just yet.

'Bess got stuck on the way here. She's with Gramps and Celeste.' Probably best to leave the part where Bess's car had rolled down an embankment for later.

'Really?' The observation had the required effect, and Granny June's attention switched from Sam. 'The snow's not that deep, is it? Although the weather forecast says we'll be getting more.'

'Engine trouble, probably. Shall we give her a call so you can speak to her? She'll be worrying about you.'

CHAPTER THREE

JUST AS SAM was finishing a more thorough examination of Granny June, the ambulance arrived, the crews clearly busy from injuries caused by the worsening weather conditions. It was agreed that they would take Granny June to the hospital, for X-rays on her ankle and to check a minor swelling that had appeared on her elbow, and Bess and her husband Tom appeared as Eloise was getting ready to go with Granny June.

'We got here as soon as we could.' Bess was reassured now, by the quiet preparations and Sam's easy manner. 'Your grandfather and Celeste are at our place, babysitting.'

Eloise smiled at the thought. 'No doubt Gramps is having a whale of a time playing with all of Aaron's toys.'

'He and Celeste were lining up for a fight with his superheroes when we left. Thank you so much, Eloise. I dread to think what could have happened if she'd been out there any longer...'

Eloise hugged her friend. 'Then don't. Granny June's okay, and that's all that matters. You're going with her in the ambulance?'

'Yes, Tom will follow in his car, and we'll bring Gran back to our place afterwards.'

'That's good. Time for you to go, now...' Sam was helping the ambulance crew carry Granny June out of the house, and Eloise pressed the door keys into Bess's hand.

'Thank you.' There was time for one last hug and then Bess hurried out to the ambulance.

Tom closed up the cottage, shaking their hands and thanking them, before climbing into his car. It was snowing more heavily now, large flakes dancing in the pools of light along the road. Eloise heaved a sigh, stopping to look.

'It's like a chocolate box, isn't it?' Sam came to stand beside her, gesturing an acknowledgement of Tom's wave.

Somewhere along the way she'd lost that. The idea that, on a picture-perfect snowy evening, doors and windows could conceal just warmth and peace. Ever since betrayal and deceit had become a part of her life, it had seemed that it must be everywhere.

'Yes. It's a very pretty part of the world.' Maybe she should trust Sam's assessment of *this* situation as well, even if it did seem much harder than trusting his medical judgement.

'Where will they take June? Is it far?'

'No, they'll be taking her to the Community Hospital, it's only a few miles away. They have X-ray facilities, and can keep her in overnight if there's any cause for concern.'

Sam nodded. 'Might be the best thing. She had a shock, and she was very cold by the time we got to her.'

It was Eloise's turn not to think about what *might* have happened. If she hadn't seen Bess's car, or if Sam hadn't decided to come with her to the village…

'Thank you. For being there.'

He smiled, brushing a snowflake from her hair in a sudden gesture that could mean anything. Maybe he hadn't quite switched off yet, from the tender care that he'd shown for Granny June.

'I'm glad I was. You're close to June and Bess?'

Why did that feel like an opportunity to apologise to him, when it was just a question? She'd acted professionally, despite all of her fears for Granny June. Gramps had been right, she did apologise too often, and turning

over a new leaf might just as well start with
Sam as anyone.

'Yes. My mother died shortly after I was
born, and I used to come up and stay with
Gramps and my grandmother during the
school holidays. Bess and I used to come here
and play a lot.'

He nodded. 'I'm sorry to hear about your
mother.'

It was more of a yearning than anything
else. For someone who would belong to her
and would support her come what may.

'Gran filled in for her really well. You
know, teenage advice and what to do about
boys…' Maybe Sam didn't want to hear about
that. He was Celeste's nephew, after all.

'You must miss her.'

Eloise puffed out a breath, which hung in
the air between them until the wind caught it
and blew it away.

'I miss her. Gramps was devastated when
she died, but the one thing that the two of
them always used to say is that life goes on.'
She turned to Sam. 'I'm really happy to see
him with Celeste. They're good together.'

Sam nodded. 'How does your father feel
about it? If you don't mind my asking.'

'My father remarried and went to Indone-
sia eight years ago. He and his wife have two

young children and they take up most of their attention.'

'He's not expressed an opinion, then?'

'Not that I've heard.' Eloise had tried to keep in contact with her father, but there had always been some excuse about why he couldn't come to the phone or make a video call, and slowly they'd drifted apart. She'd felt angry and neglected, and then she'd come to terms with the loss, because moving on was one of those things that wasn't always a choice.

Maybe the cold shiver that ran down her spine was because they were standing outside in the snow. Maybe because Sam's questions reminded her that she was alone in life, with only Gramps to protect her. Or maybe it was because the warmth in his eyes seemed to hold the kind of understanding that she craved.

'It's cold out here. We should get home...' She grabbed at the first, most obvious, explanation rather than contemplate the other two.

He nodded, pulling his keys from his pocket. 'Want to drive?'

It was an obvious tease, and she didn't need to feel grateful that he'd even considered the possibility of giving his car keys back to her. Eloise shot him a smile and headed for the passenger door.

* * *

It had occurred to Sam that there was still time to run.

The more time he spent with Eloise, the more he was fascinated by her. Her vulnerability, and how she seemed so alone and hurt. Her warmth and the way she'd cared for her friends. And the way her strength had suddenly shown itself, when it was needed. That had been the biggest turn-on of all, and in allowing himself to even think that way Sam was stepping into the same dangerous territory he'd inhabited with Alice.

It wouldn't be so difficult to manufacture an excuse about being needed at his practice in London, Paul and Aunt Celeste would insist that he went. It was looking increasingly as if the party wasn't going to happen, and by tomorrow he might find that it wasn't so easy to go anywhere.

Instead, he took off his coat. Eloise was drawing the curtains, stopping to look out of the sitting room window.

'Do you have to be back at work on Monday morning?'

Sam shook his head. 'No, I'm not due back at the surgery until next Wednesday.'

She nodded, smiling. 'That's good. If this keeps up the roads might be blocked over the weekend, but they're usually cleared within a couple of days. It would be awkward to be stranded up here if you had to work.'

Not quite as awkward as things were now, trying to navigate his way through all of the uncertainties. All of the things that challenged his peace of mind and made him feel that he wanted things that he'd already decided he couldn't have. But Eloise's smile, and her apparent pleasure that he wasn't going to be driving back to London this evening outweighed all of that.

They were both hungry, and there was enough food in the kitchen to feed an army. Eloise went for quick and easy, and half an hour later they sat down at the kitchen table to sausages and mash. One bite was enough to indicate that Eloise hadn't sacrificed taste for speed.

'These sausages are great. And the onion gravy's *got* to be a secret recipe…' He couldn't help grinning at her. Eloise's response to praise was always a glowing smile, as if she hadn't expected anyone to notice all of the effort she put into things.

'The sausages are from one of the farms in the area. And yes, the onion gravy's a secret recipe so don't ask me for it.'

'You've put a lot of work into this weekend.'

This time she blushed a little. 'I wanted everything to be perfect for Gramps and Celeste.'

'Things haven't quite gone to plan so far, but it's not been so bad, has it? When I called Aunt Celeste just now to see how they were doing, she said they were having a wonderful time and that she couldn't stop and talk because your grandfather was putting Aaron's train set together. Apparently her supervision is an all-important part of the process.'

Eloise chuckled. 'They have a lot of fun together. I just hope that everything's going to be all right tomorrow…'

That doubt again. As if disaster was always waiting, just around the corner.

'Whatever happens, it'll be fine. We'll make it so, eh?'

She hesitated and then smiled. 'Yes. Thanks.'

They ate in silence, too hungry for much conversation, and then Eloise leaned back in her seat, toying with the last sausage on her plate. 'You and Celeste are very close, aren't you?'

Sam nodded, as he swallowed his last mouthful of food. 'Yes. She did a lot for me and my brother and sister when our parents' marriage broke up. Provided us with a safe place away from all the conflict. It was a very messy break-up.'

'I didn't realise. I shouldn't have mentioned it…' Eloise had secrets and she should respect that Sam might well not want to talk about this.

'It's okay, it's all ancient history. I was thirteen when my parents split up, and it had been coming for as long as I can remember. My father wouldn't accept that my mother wanted to leave him, and he started stalking and harassing her. He'd turn up at the house at all hours of the day and night, and in the end she had to take out a restraining order. Aunt Celeste did the one thing that no one else did and kept speaking to both sides.' He stretched his arms, rubbing the back of his head. 'She spoke her mind, of course. Didn't pull any punches.'

'Pulling punches doesn't seem much like Celeste's style.'

That made him laugh, only there was a trace of bitterness there. Eloise wondered if the sudden haunted look in his eyes mirrored that of her own. It wasn't pleasant to watch.

'It's not her style at all. She loved my father, he was her brother. But she had no hesitation in telling him that he had to stay away from my mother, or in supporting Mum in a practical sense. Or trying to get my father to take some help when he started drinking. I was nineteen when he died, and Aunt Celeste was devastated.'

'I'm so sorry. That must have been a very difficult loss for both of you.'

'There were a lot of missed opportunities, but you can't force someone to take help when they don't want it. His liver began to fail but he wouldn't give up drinking. Aunt Celeste helped me come to terms with that too.'

The hurt in his face belied his assertion that this was all in the past. Those wounds still remained, and maybe they always would. Sam was living with something as well, and that made it even more necessary for her to keep some kind of emotional distance while they were trapped in such close proximity to each other. His peace of mind seemed as fragile as hers was.

But she couldn't help it. She wanted to acknowledge the chaos and pain of his childhood, and her feelings must be showing in her face. Sam's gaze caught hers, and she saw the lines of tension in his brow soften. He gave a little nod, as if he'd seen her thoughts.

'Thank you. It's all a long time ago now.'

It was an effort to break that sweet connection, but Sam clearly didn't want to say any more. Eloise got to her feet, leaning towards him to pick up his plate.

'Would you like some dessert?'

He shook his head. 'Thanks...but shall we wait until Paul and Aunt Celeste are home?'

Gramps had called, saying that Granny June had been released from hospital with a badly sprained ankle, and that she'd be staying with Bess and Tom while she recovered. They'd be home in half an hour.

While Eloise set to work making dinner for them, Sam was making his own preparations. He disappeared into the scullery and she heard him opening and closing drawers and cupboards, obviously looking for something. Before she could go and see what he was doing he reappeared, holding candles, napkins and silver cutlery.

'I thought we'd eat in here, it's warmer than the dining room...'

He nodded, starting to arrange the candles at the centre of one end of the long table. 'Yeah, that's what I thought too. No reason not to make it nice, eh?'

Eloise smiled. He'd said that he'd help to make the weekend a success, whatever happened, and that clearly wasn't an empty promise. 'Shall we break out the champagne, then?'

He thought for a moment and then nodded. 'Champagne with bangers and mash. I like your style.'

By the time she heard Gramps and Celeste at the front door, the champagne was chilling in an ice bucket. Crystal glasses shone in the candlelight and the bangers and mash was ready to be served on the best plates.

'It looks great.' She took a moment to survey the table. 'You said you'd make things nice for Gramps and Celeste...'

Something flickered in his eyes, the warmth greater than even candlelight could achieve. 'What makes you think it's for them? This is for you.'

She caught her breath, but Sam was already gone, out into the hallway to hang up the coats and shepherd Gramps and Celeste through to the kitchen. Hugging the thought that he'd done this for her against her chest like a warm, comforting blanket, she turned back to the range to start serving the food.

There were exclamations of delight from Celeste, along with Gramps' quiet chuckle of approval. Eloise and Sam sat with them at the table, sipping champagne and eating nibbles while Gramps and Celeste tucked into their meal. It was impossible not to feel that Sam was watching her, and when Eloise turned and mouthed *Thank you* he smiled.

There was ice-cream for dessert, and then they repaired to the sitting room, taking their glasses with them while Eloise prepared coffee. When she brought the tray in, Gramps smilingly got to his feet.

'I think this is the right time for my speech, don't you, Celeste?'

'Absolutely, Paul.' Celeste beamed at him in anticipation, although she must already know what he intended to say. 'Let's hear it.'

'Don't you want to wait until everyone's here?' Gramps' speech had been scheduled for the dinner on Friday evening, which had been planned to welcome everyone.

'We're here, Eloise,' Gramps chided her gently. 'I think *this* is the time for it.'

Sam had topped up everyone's glasses and Aunt Celeste had once again pronounced herself *all ears*. Paul took two folded sheets of paper from the mantelpiece, and then stood to one side of the hearth.

Sam had been in the audience for more than one of Dr Paul Grant's lectures, and he normally spoke fluently and entertainingly, without even glancing at his notes. But this time he seemed almost nervous, studying the paper in his hand.

'Come along, darling. Out with it…' Aunt Celeste came to the rescue as usual, flashing Paul with an expectant smile. He laughed, putting the paper into his pocket.

'A toast first. To Celeste, whose questionable judgement has led her to agree to marry me. I'm looking forward to many more years of bad decisions together, darling.'

'Absolutely!' Aunt Celeste laughed and took a sip of her champagne. 'And to Paul, who always knows how to lead a woman astray.'

Bad decisions and leading each other astray suited them both very well. So well, in fact, that it was tempting to make a bad decision all of his own.

Another bad decision. The one to make this meal a little special hadn't been so bad, that was fun for everyone. Telling Eloise that it had been all for her hadn't been such a smart move, but it was the truth. She seemed to take every disruption of the plans for the coming weekend so much to heart, and her sudden smile had been so delicious that it was hard to bring himself to regret anything.

The champagne was making his head swim. Or maybe that was just watching her, as she took a sip from her glass. Or being caught watching her, as her gaze found his and a smile sprang to her lips before she looked quickly away again.

Sam turned his attention to Paul, who was already getting on with the first part of his speech.

'The year is now 1802, and two young men are fresh-faced students at medical school. Aloysius Grant and Henry Douglas became firm friends. The opportunity to quarrel over women never presented itself, in fact it's said that Aloysius went to some lengths to engineer Henry's introduction to his future wife. They were young, had all of the advantages that money could provide, and in learning together how to be of service to others a deep affection had been born. What could go wrong...?'

Every member of the Grant and Douglas families knew what *had* gone wrong. Paul launched into the story of how Aloysius Grant had written a medical paper, which Henry Douglas had debunked. The subsequent quarrel in the medical press had soured their relationship.

'They'd been inseparable friends, and maybe that was why they argued so bitterly, and never reconciled...' Paul gave a regretful smile at the ways of the world, and Sam felt his heart jump, as if this story really was something that was new and shocking. Maybe he should take it as a cautionary tale. If you didn't get too close to someone, then you couldn't do so much damage to each other. Sam suspected that his history and Eloise's were an explosive mix, and that they could do a great deal of damage together.

'Thirty years later when their old alma mater, here in Norfolk, was looking to grow, alumni were invited to contribute to new residences for students. Both Aloysius and Henry responded to the call, but only because each wanted to shame the other. Grant College and Douglas College were built and they still stand today, their sporting and academic rivalry a memorial to two foolish men, who each wanted to outdo the other.'

Eloise was smiling as she turned to Sam. 'You were at Douglas College?'

Sam hadn't felt much like following in his father's footsteps when he'd gone to medical school, and he hadn't changed his mind about that since. He shook his head.

'No, I broke with tradition and studied down in London. But there was that one rugby match I rather wished I hadn't been involved in…' He turned the corners of his mouth down.

Aunt Celeste chuckled. 'I thought I did rather a good job on your nose, Sam. Are you telling me you don't like it?'

'You did a fine job. It's far better than it was before, but I didn't much like being punched in the face by the Grant team's scrum half.'

Paul was chuckling. 'I seem to remember there was some concern over there having been a ringer on the team.'

Aunt Celeste's eyebrows shot up. 'Vitriol, more like! Sam's a Grant, isn't he? So he can play for the team even if he's not a member of Grant College. I'd like to know what happened to the lad who was supposed to be playing…'

Paul and Aunt Celeste were teasing each other amicably and Sam turned to Eloise, his smile suddenly dying on his lips. Her cheeks were pink with embarrassment and she looked as if she wanted the cushions of the armchair she was sitting in to swallow her up.

There was no opportunity to ask her to explain, not now at least, because Paul had launched into an account of his and Celeste's progression from rivals to complete and loving accord. Another toast was proposed, to a new era of harmony between the Grants and the Douglases, and all four of them drained their glasses.

Then Eloise seemed to see an opportunity for escape and, before Sam could think of anything to say that might stop her, she was on her feet, collecting the empty cups and glasses and heading for the kitchen.

CHAPTER FOUR

A LITTLE TRICKLE of discomfort had run down Eloise's spine when Sam had mentioned the rugby match. It had turned into a gush of agonised embarrassment when she realised it had been *that* rugby match. And he had been *that* player.

She could come clean to him later, when Gramps and Celeste weren't around. In the meantime, the kitchen seemed like a good hiding place.

Eloise stiffened as she heard someone enter the kitchen. The old flagstones were an early warning system, and it was possible to know who was there from the sound of their footsteps. By the time she'd turned from the sink she'd managed to compose herself.

He'd made no pretence of carrying something through from the sitting room, and was looking at her silently. Eloise swallowed down the impulse to apologise, because that wasn't going to deflect him.

'I…didn't realise that you were there at that rugby match.'

'I didn't realise *you* were.'

Eloise studied the flagstones at her feet. 'Actually, I wasn't. I was…somewhere else.'

That wasn't going to deflect him either. Sam was clearly one of those people who only became more curious in the face of things he didn't understand.

'Where?' He asked the inevitable question and she couldn't help meeting his gaze. Fair enough, maybe it was better that she came clean.

'In the boathouse. With the missing members of the Douglas College rugby team.'

His grin broadened. 'You…what? Charmed them away from the match?'

'No! That wouldn't have worked anyway. Rag week had just finished and Douglas College had been playing some pretty mean tricks on us. You really don't want to know what they did to the plumbing in the girls' bathrooms.' Eloise decided that elaborating any further sounded as if she was trying to justify herself.

'Aunt Celeste told me about that. Sounds pretty vile.' He was *still* grinning.

'Well, anyway. Feelings were running high, and we decided to pay them back. Two of their best players used to go running together and… I pretended I'd fallen on the path through the woods and broken my leg.'

He chuckled. 'Okay, I've got it. No doubt you were pretty convincing since you would have known exactly what a broken leg looked like, and when the rugby players stopped to help, a gang from Grant College jumped out at them. Probably tied them up, put them in the back of a van.'

'Car. We were gentle with them. And we didn't have to tie them up, they were outnumbered so they just came with us.' He was making this sound a lot worse than it had actually been.

'I'm disappointed.' His grin didn't look disappointed at all. 'I have a picture of you executing a precise military operation.'

'It was nothing of the kind. We took them to the boathouse and gave them coffee and sandwiches.'

'So it was the most benign kidnapping ever. And I was the only casualty, after getting in the way when one of the Grant College team threw a punch in response to my being brought into the team when I wasn't strictly speaking anything to do with Douglas College and shouldn't have been playing for them.'

'Yes. I'm really sorry.' Eloise reckoned that an apology probably was in order for that.

He shrugged. 'You weren't the one who punched me. And Aunt Celeste fixed it.'

'It looks…great.' Maybe she shouldn't comment on that it was far too tempting to widen the parameters and tell him that everything about him was wonderful. 'I knew that those rugby matches were pretty hard fought, and I should have thought of the consequences of my actions a bit more carefully.'

Sam laughed. 'Hindsight's always twenty-twenty, I guess. I tell myself that when I browse through my own extensive catalogue of mistakes.'

He was trying to make her feel better. That was nice of him, but there was a downward quirk of his lips that made her wonder if Sam too was haunted by his mistakes.

'Would you like something else to drink? We have everything from hot chocolate to four different kinds of fruit juice.'

'Thanks, but no. I'm going to get an early night.'

That should have come as a relief. No more fighting with herself to ignore the warmth of his gaze. No more agonising over finding a way to tell him that it would be better for them both if they ignored whatever it was that was going on between them.

That was probably the best reason of all why sitting down at the kitchen table and having a heart-to-heart over mugs of hot chocolate really shouldn't happen. By tomorrow, sleep would have given her a better perspective on all of this.

Eloise smiled at him, filling the sink to rinse the glasses. 'Sleep well, then.'

Sam hadn't slept very well. A strange bed, and a house that seemed to creak around him every time there was the slightest movement. And Eloise. Determined and resourceful and yet so vulnerable. Somehow, he couldn't just let it go…

Maybe it would defuse the attraction that sparked between them if he was a bit more candid. Told her that he knew she'd been through a bad break-up and that he had too. Then they'd both know where they stood, and they could enjoy each other's company in the knowledge that there would be nothing more between them. But, on the other hand…a conversation like that might be construed as a prelude to intimacy.

In the early hours of the morning his brain

must have suddenly switched off, overwhelmed by so many conflicting thoughts. When he drowsily awoke the next morning it was late.

Eloise was sitting with Paul and Aunt Celeste in the kitchen, and he made for the coffee machine.

'The weekend's off,' Aunt Celeste announced with a smile.

'You're not disappointed?' There it was again. That wish to defend Eloise and acknowledge everything she'd done to make the weekend a success.

'Of course I am. If you'd been up a bit earlier you would have known that, Eloise has put in so much work. But there's nothing anyone can do about it. Paul's been on the phone to everyone and they've all decided against travelling up here. The weather forecast says more snow this afternoon.'

Sam looked out of the window. The snow still wasn't too deep, but any more and things would be grinding to a halt.

'Seems sensible. So what *are* you happy about?'

'It appears that we've got something else to be getting our teeth into. Paul's had a call from the local Community Hospital, who were wondering if we were available to help out if needed. We're going over there this morning to talk to their head of services. Are you in?'

Aunt Celeste knew she didn't need to ask. 'I'm in. Just let me grab some breakfast first…'

He only had time to gulp down half a cup of coffee. Paul and Aunt Celeste had already put on their coats and were outside clearing his car of snow, having decided that it would be the best to take in these conditions. Eloise smilingly went to the range cooker, opening up the warming compartment and withdrawing a bacon sandwich on a plate.

'I made this when I heard you moving around upstairs. I can either fight Gramps and Celeste off while you take a minute to eat it, or I'll wrap it up and you can take it with you.'

'You'll drive?'

She smiled. 'Yes, I'll drive.'

Clearly she was in determined mode this morning, and none of Sam's good intentions from last night could resist that. He went to fetch their coats and his car keys and when he returned to the kitchen Eloise had a foil-wrapped package for him, and a full travel cup of coffee.

'Thanks.'

Eloise pulled on her coat, taking a purple knitted hat out of the pocket and pulling it down over her ears. It looked just as charming as the red one she'd worn yesterday. 'Let's go then, before Gramps and Celeste explode from impatience...'

The Community Hospital was a large one-storey building with a pitched slate roof, which blended into the countryside around it. A couple of ambulances were parked on one side of the building, and as they entered the welcoming reception area a man in a sweater stepped forward, shaking Paul's hand.

'Thanks for coming, Paul.' He turned to Celeste. 'You're Ms Douglas?'

'Celeste, please. Plastic surgeon, although I can turn my hand to most things.'

'And this is my granddaughter, Eloise Grant. She works in an Accident and Emergency department in London. And Sam Douglas is a GP.'

'Thanks, that's marvellous. I'm Joe Parrish and I'm co-ordinating the volunteers. We're managing right now, but with more snow on the way we may be cut off from the main hospital, that's been an issue for us before. In that eventuality we'll have to deal with all the cases from this area that would normally go there, and so we'll need all the help we can get.'

'You deal with ambulance cases already, don't you?' Sam remembered that June had been brought here yesterday.

'Yes, we do, we have X-ray and scanning capabilities and we can deal with a wide range of minor injuries. We also have a couple of ambulances based here, which will take more serious cases over to the A&E department in the main hospital. We've already experienced an uptick in the number of people coming in, due to the weather conditions, but, as I say, we're managing well at the moment. But we're preparing to take in more if needs be. I'd appreciate any input you have on the planning side, Paul.'

Paul nodded. 'Of course. Maybe I can show the others around a bit first? Just so they know what they're letting themselves in for...'

There was a sizeable waiting area that was busy but nowhere near full at the moment, with several treatment rooms along one side. Paul led them along a short corridor and punched an entry code into a door, which opened onto another large space which looked as if it was currently being repurposed, examination beds lined up along one side and curtains being hung to make semi-private treatment areas.

'This is usually used for various different clinics, but it doubles up nicely as an overflow area for emergencies.'

Eloise was looking around, checking on the equipment available. 'Defibrillators?'

Paul nodded. 'You'll have everything you need. That's what I'm going to be discussing with Joe.'

She grinned suddenly. 'So I don't need to make a list, eh, Gramps?'

Paul chuckled. 'Not unless there's something you've discovered for yourself, since I taught you everything I know.'

Eloise snorted with laughter. 'No, I'm still waiting for a chance to put some of the things you taught me into practice. Give me another ten years…'

The trust between them was clear. Sam had seen yesterday that she was confident and effective when it came to her work, and yet she was so very vulnerable in her private life. Whatever the circumstances of the cancelled marriage that Aunt Celeste had described to him, they must have hurt Eloise very badly.

Eloise and Paul were still talking together and Sam's attention was drawn back to the conversation by the mention of his name.

'What do you think, Sam? We'll go back to the house and Gramps and Celeste will stay here to help Joe?'

'Uh…if there's nothing for us to do here. Just give me a call and I'll come back and collect you both, but don't leave it too late. You don't want to be stuck here.'

'Best place for us in the circumstances,' Aunt Celeste retorted. 'And anyway there's always Ted.'

Eloise smiled. 'Yes, there's always Ted. Don't forget to be back before six, because I'm cooking.'

As they walked out to the car together, Sam asked the obvious question. 'Who's Ted?'

'He's one of the local farmers. He has a motor sled that he uses on the farm when it snows—not one of those sporty one-person models, this one's ex-army and a real workhorse of a machine, it'll take four passengers easily. He phoned this morning before you were up, and said that if we needed to go into the hospital to help out we should just call him.'

'Sounds like a very handy person to know in the circumstances.'

'Yes, he is. The sled's great, I think that Celeste's rather hoping they'll be staying long enough to need it.'

'And meanwhile…what are we going to be doing?' Sam was pretty sure that Eloise had a plan.

'Well, the welcome dinner was supposed to be this evening. We haven't got any people but we do have plenty of food. And, of course, the happy couple to contend with.'

'Ah. So we're making the best of things. For them and for us?' He wondered whether Eloise would take the step of claiming some enjoyment for herself.

Her fingers brushed his as she handed him his car keys, and he saw her cheeks flush. 'If I cook then maybe you'll take care of the table?'

And maybe, like last night, she'd accept that some of that was for her and not just Paul and Aunt Celeste.

'Okay. That sounds fair. Are we going to dress for dinner?'

'Yes, I thought so.'

Sam nodded, trying not to wonder what Eloise would be wearing. This was *really* sounding like a plan.

Eloise was almost glad that no one was going to be turning up for the weekend. Given the choice, she'd rather be at the hospital, helping out, than having to contend with her whole family, together in one room. And Sam had a way of making everything special.

He followed her into the kitchen, hanging his coat on the back of one of the chairs. Sam's smile seemed so much more potent when they were alone together and Eloise tried to ignore it.

'We were going to have Beef Wellington, so that's easy enough. I can put all of the extras into the freezer and just cook one of them for tonight. I can freeze the extra vegetables as well, and just cook enough for four.'

'There'll be enough room in the freezer?' Sam regarded the fridge-freezer in the corner of the kitchen.

'There are two big chest freezers in the pantry; there's plenty of room there. We'll be having green beans with garlic, thyme and white wine, Brussels sprouts with chestnuts and bacon and roasted asparagus. Along with mashed potatoes and a hollandaise sauce.'

He nodded. 'Sounds delicious. You obviously have everything well in hand.'

In the kitchen...yes. Everywhere else...not even close.

'There is one other problem. You've seen the Great Hall?'

'Aunt Celeste showed me around the house when I first came up here for the weekend, to meet your grandfather.' He shot her a querying look. 'We're eating there?'

'That was the original plan, the Great Hall's always been Gramps' favourite place in the house. But I think that we should probably move to the dining room.'

'You like the Great Hall?'

He always asked the most difficult questions. 'Yes, I like it. It has a real sense of occasion about it.'

'Then we'll do it there.'

No amount of moving furniture was going to make the Great Hall into an intimate space for four people.

'What do you have in mind?'

Sam started to walk out into the hallway and Eloise called him back, motioning to the door at the other end of the kitchen. All of the rooms in the house had more than one door, which made things confusing at times, but followed the Tudor practice of having rooms leading from one to the other.

There was a chill in the air in the Great Hall, which made her shiver. That was another problem. It needed to be full of people to warm up to a comfortable temperature for sitting and eating. Sam was looking around, inspecting the windows that ran along the length of the hall on one side, the massive inglenook that contained a glass-fronted stove on the other and the long oak table that was placed in the centre of the room.

'This can go over there. And we can use that smaller table.' He pointed towards the far end of the hall, where a smaller serving table stood against the wall.

'Yes.' Eloise wasn't sure how that was going to work, it would just make the empty space look even more cavernous. But she supposed that since she'd asked Sam to help she should at least sound a little positive. 'The big table comes apart, I can help you move it.'

'That's okay, I'll manage. And if we sit by the fireplace it'll be warm enough there?'

'Yes, I suppose so. But isn't it going to feel as if we're huddled around the fire with this massive space around us?'

Sam smiled suddenly. 'Will you leave it with me?'

Trust him. She could do that, if all he had in mind was moving furniture around.

'Okay. I'll prepare myself for a surprise.'

'I'm aiming for delight, actually.'

Okay, so delight was a lot more confronting. But… She couldn't say no, the thought was far too tempting. And suddenly, delight was something she missed very much.

'I'll look forward to seeing what you come up with.'

CHAPTER FIVE

ELOISE HAD KEPT herself to the kitchen, which wasn't difficult because there was plenty to do, wrapping all of the extra food for the freezer and then preparing the food for tonight. Everything was ready to go into the oven, and when it did she would have time to dress for dinner and then serve everything without too much rushing around.

At three the sky began to darken with cloud, and Sam appeared in the kitchen doorway again. 'Paul's just called and I'm going to pick them up. I won't be long.'

'Shall I come too? Just in case they need us.'

'Paul says that they've reworked the rotas and they have enough staff coming in early to cover tonight, so we'll only be in the way. It's tomorrow when they'll most likely be calling us in.'

'Okay. So what do you think about getting

a bottle of wine up from the cellar to warm up to room temperature?'

He pressed his lips together, weighing up the idea. 'I suppose…it might be better to stick to soft drinks. You never know what's going to happen. Maybe we can work on creating an intoxicating atmosphere.'

An evening spent just for the sheer pleasure of the company you were in. Eloise had forgotten how long it had been since she'd done that and right now it seemed an act of stupid self-denial to reject it.

'I'll look forward to it.'

He returned an hour later, and Eloise heard Gramps and Celeste chatting together animatedly as they climbed the stairs. Then Sam reappeared in the doorway, taking off his coat.

'Seems we just made it in time. It's starting to snow heavily now. I've sent Paul and Aunt Celeste upstairs and told them they're not to come back down again until we're ready. Apparently they've plenty to do, they're halfway through a chess game.'

'Ah, the chess game. Did you know that when Celeste's down in London they play by text?'

He chuckled. 'No, I didn't know that.'

'Gramps sends roses every time Celeste wins a game. I think he loses on purpose sometimes.' Eloise had never thought about it much before, but now it seemed an incurably romantic gesture.

'They're starting to make me feel very old and staid.'

'Me too.' Perhaps a little of the happiness was rubbing off. Eloise could almost feel the sparkle in the air. But that sparkle and the accompanying warmth seemed to revolve entirely around Sam.

'I'd better get on. Give me a call when you want me to watch dinner so you can go and dress.'

'Thanks. That won't be for another hour…'

When she heard Sam climbing the stairs and reckoned that he'd gone to dress for dinner, the temptation to sneak into the Great Hall and take a look was almost irresistible. But Eloise had promised not to, and she had enough to do to occupy her time. And then Sam appeared, wearing an evening suit. The dark waistcoat and tie emphasised his broad frame and handsome features, bringing a whole new meaning to the word *temptation*.

'You scrub up pretty well, Dr Douglas.' Acknowledge it. Get it out in the open. Then it couldn't hurt her.

'Thanks.' The surprise in his tone only

added to the temptation. Most gorgeous men knew it, but if Sam did then he had no time for the idea. Eloise shouldn't have any time for it either. She was already walking a tight-rope, allowing herself to take more pleasure in his company than she should. But some-how that danger only added to the excitement of allowing herself to feel attracted to him.

'Are you going to show me what you've done in the Great Hall now?'

He nodded, holding out his arm in a sig-nal that she should take it. Eloise wiped her hands and took her apron off, rather sheep-ishly taking his arm.

And then, suddenly, she felt like a million dollars. As if her hair wasn't tied back in a scrunchie, and she hadn't been working all afternoon in the kitchen. He smiled down at her as if she were Cinderella, after her fairy godmother was through with her. He was def-initely the handsome prince.

It was impossible not to hang a little more tightly onto his arm, because she could smell the scent of soap, which immediately conjured up visions of Sam showering.

When he opened the door to the Great Hall, escorting her inside, the fairy tale started to become real. Almost too real—reminding her that the romance of it all was beyond her aspirations now.

The subtle electric lighting, that was used to supplement the flickering candlelight from the chandeliers, had been turned off. Sam had lit the stove, and a warm glow spread across the smaller dining table that he'd placed in front of the inglenook. Two large candelabra stood on the table, each surrounded by flowers, and the surplus blooms spilled over the stone mantelpiece above the inglenook.

A pure white cloth. Sparkling silver and crystal glassware. It was simple, elegant and, since the rest of the hall was in shadow, it was intimate as well, as if they were gathered around a campfire in the darkness. To add a touch of magic, Sam had obviously found the solar lights in the storeroom and planted them outside the windows, and they illuminated the flakes of snow that were falling now.

'Sam, it's beautiful! Gramps and Celeste are going to love it.'

'What matters to me is whether you like it.' The flickering candlelight seemed to caress his face. Why wouldn't it? Light could go anywhere it pleased.

Eloise felt her breath catch in her throat, tears pricking at the sides of her eyes, at all that she'd lost. Turning away from him, she pretended to examine the flowers at each side of the hearth, putting one that had been dislodged back into place.

Somehow, she managed to face him again. To smile and pretend that she was just very impressed, and not completely overwhelmed that he'd done all of this for her.

'It's really beautiful, Sam. I love it.'

She had to go now, before she made a fool of herself. Eloise made a hurried excuse about having to go and get dressed for dinner now and then, like Cinderella, she ran from the Prince Charming that she could never have.

Sam sat at the kitchen table, fiddling with his phone. He'd restlessly checked the contents of the oven and reviewed Eloise's list and, just as she'd informed him, there was nothing he needed to do.

Which was a shame, because it left his mind entirely free to wander. Celeste and Paul didn't really need any more romance in their lives; they had it already. He'd started out trying to make a special evening for Eloise, and ended up making it for himself as well. Wondering how she might look in soft, flickering candlelight. How she might smile when she saw the result of his efforts, knowing that it would make his own heart beat faster. A heart that seemed to have slowed to monotonous regularity since Alice had left him.

He'd tried. Tried to leave the doubts and the fears behind, tried to be nothing like his father, who had asked only for what he'd wanted and disregarded everyone else's wishes. Sam had thought he'd succeeded, learning how to take a breath—sometimes more than one—and suppress his anger when it threatened to blind him to other people's wants and needs. He'd approached his relationships carefully and thoughtfully, the break-ups with particular care. Alice had been the exception to that. When she'd refused to tell him why she was leaving he couldn't dismiss his anger and when he'd felt it seep through into his reactions, heard its edge in his own voice... It had shocked him how much like his father he'd sounded.

So he'd let Alice go. Sam had moved on, the way his father should have done, never acknowledging any pain. In the year between then and now, he'd hardly even noticed how grey his life had become.

And then Eloise had reminded him all about colour and excitement and uncertainty. About the thrill of not being able to get someone out of your head. Even the sound of her footsteps, outside in the hall, made all of his senses switch to high alert. And when she appeared in the doorway his heart jumped.

'You look great.'

Eloise was wearing a bottle-green velvet dress. Plain, with three-quarter length sleeves and a hem that fell almost to her ankles, with high strappy silver sandals. The colour suited her dark hair, which was piled up on top of her head, and the dress showed off her figure. Great didn't really cover it—she looked breathtaking.

'Thank you.' Maybe his expression had indicated breathtaking, because Sam thought he saw a blush steal across her cheeks. Then she turned away, bending to peer into the oven.

He couldn't keep his eyes off her. The way she moved, and how she seemed to take the light with her everywhere she went. He couldn't keep his mind off wanting her to be happy, which was already morphing into a wish to be the one who made her happy.

'I think everything's ready…'

'I'll serve up, shall I? You can go and fetch Paul and Aunt Celeste.' Their reaction when they saw the table laden with food would be a few more grains of happiness to scatter at her feet.

She hesitated and then smiled. 'Okay, thanks.'

Sam saw her straighten, smoothing her hands across her dress as she walked out of the kitchen, as if she'd been chosen to escort royal guests into the Great Hall. Paul and Aunt Celeste were more important to her than a king and his queen, and he smiled.

Silence, as he made the first journey to the table and back. As Sam was picking up the serving dishes, ready to make the second, he heard a little scream echoing in from the Great Hall. Aunt Celeste was adding her seal of approval to the evening. When he walked back to the table, she was hugging Eloise tight.

'This looks great, Sam, thank you.' Paul shot him a broad grin. 'I don't use the Hall unless there are a lot of guests, but I see I've been missing something.'

'Sam's good at that kind of thing.' Aunt Celeste shot him a look that made it clear she approved of his efforts. 'And Eloise... The food smells absolutely marvellous. Thank you so much...'

The glasses were filled, and they sat down to eat. Sam had put Celeste and Paul at either end of the table and, to avoid anyone having their back to the heat of the fire, he and Eloise were sitting next to each other, facing the hearth. That had been a mistake. Sam would have borne the discomfort of the fire at his back for the chance to look up at Eloise.

She was glowing. The rich fabric of her dress failed to draw his attention away from the way her face shone in the firelight. And he could steal glances to his left, bask in the pleasure that she was clearly taking in the meal.

It was a feast fit for a king. When the first course was finished, Paul leaned back in his seat, smiling. 'What do you say we take a little break before dessert?'

That seemed to be a signal for Celeste to reach for her evening bag. 'Good idea.' She withdrew a gold-wrapped package. 'Eloise, this is for you. I wish there had been more people here, to applaud everything you've done to make this weekend such a joy for us, but we'll have to do.'

Eloise looked genuinely taken aback. When she didn't take the package, Celeste got to her feet, pressing it into her hand.

'I didn't…' She turned towards Sam, her cheeks burning. 'Sam did everything in here.'

'And you've been working hard everywhere else for days, darling,' Celeste reprimanded her. 'Anyway, this really isn't going to suit Sam.'

Sam chuckled, picking up his glass. 'To

Eloise. Thank you for making this evening wonderful.'

Paul and Celeste followed suit, making the toast. But Sam could see nothing but Eloise, as she turned to him, her lips a little moist, her gaze warm in the firelight. She was the most beautiful woman he'd ever seen.

Were these just fantasies of a different life? One where he could meet someone and fall in love, without all of the hesitation and insecurity that he'd felt in the past? Sam doubted whether he was capable of constructing a fantasy like this. The way that Eloise carefully peeled the tape from the wrapping paper, flashing a mischievous smile at her grandfather, who was leaning forward, anxious to see whether she'd like her present. The curve of her cheek, flushed with the caress of the fire burning in the inglenook.

It was both delightful and challenging, but this was something real. Something he could no longer dismiss as a mere reminder of what seemed missing in his life. Eloise had not just made him notice the void, she was beginning to fill it as well.

'Oh! It's beautiful, thank you!' She withdrew a gold filigree heart on a chain from its box.

Paul and Celeste were talking, but all that

Sam could hear and see was Eloise. She fumbled behind her neck with the chain and suddenly he found himself on his feet, carefully fixing the clasp. Inhaling her scent as if it might save his life.

She turned a little, her hand on the pendant, smiling a *thank you* to Celeste and Paul. And then her gaze met his. Suddenly it felt as if they were the only two people in the room.

Sam was beginning to feel that he'd lost too much. Avoiding a nasty break-up meant avoiding having something that you wanted to keep. But he wanted to keep the longing that he felt, as Eloise's lips curved into a smile that seemed private and all for him, the wish to know her, to be able to talk about anything and share everything. He felt like a thief, stealing every last drop of romance from an evening that had never been designed to be for him and Eloise. But still, he couldn't help wanting more...

Sam had thought of everything. The fireworks that had been planned for the evening weren't going to work in the heavy snow that was falling outside, but when he fetched the dessert from the refrigerator he arranged table fireworks around it, so that when he entered the Great Hall there was a sparkling blaze of light to accompany him.

He quietly steered the evening to its close, via surprise presents from Gramps and Celeste, who had told each other that they wouldn't exchange engagement gifts but had both secretly broken the rule. Celeste had given Gramps a new watch, engraved with a loving message, which replaced the old and rather battered timepiece on his wrist. And they'd all trooped upstairs to see the room that Gramps had had decorated as Celeste's new study.

'It's so pretty, isn't it?' Eloise stopped at the large window at the top of the stairs, looking out on the falling snow. 'And such a shame that it brings so many challenges.'

Sam chuckled. 'Isn't that always the way? Maybe we shouldn't think about the challenges—they'll always be there. Just take the pleasures.'

Perhaps Sam wasn't talking just about the snow. Maybe Eloise wasn't either. Tonight did seem like one of those times when she could take the pleasures and forget about the challenges. Sam proffered his arm and she took it.

'Oh!' As she turned towards the stairs, she missed her footing on the uneven floorboards and the high heels did the rest. Suddenly she found herself in Sam's arms.

Gramps and Celeste were already downstairs and at this moment they might as well be a hundred miles away. And using this moment to feel the strong lines of his body against hers seemed like a strangely good idea.

'Did you twist your ankle?' No one had ever enquired after her health with such a delicious smile.

'No. This house really isn't made for wearing high heels.'

For a moment, he didn't seem to realise that meant he could let her go now. She felt the pressure of his arm around her waist pull her a little closer. Sam's breath caught suddenly and her own heartbeat began to race frenetically. Any moment now, it was all going to prove too much to bear.

'We should go and see what they're up to down there.' The slight quirk of his mouth, and the way he kept hold of her for just a few seconds longer, betrayed his reluctance.

'Give them a moment more together.' Give *us* a moment more… The words tripped off Eloise's tongue before she could stop them and Sam nodded.

She felt his fingers brush the back of her

hand, then encircle it loosely, raising it to his mouth. She barely felt the brush of his lips. It was a slightly old-fashioned recognition that might have been given any number of times at tonight's formal party, if more people had turned up. But the look in his eyes made it seem both intimate and exciting.

'Eloise… Sam… What are you two doing up there?' Celeste's voice broke the spell, and she came to her senses. Michael had been the one person she should have been able to trust, but he'd betrayed her. She hardly knew Sam, and kissing him now would be a bad idea. She couldn't see how that might possibly change in the foreseeable future.

'Nothing…' she called back, wondering whether Sam's thoughts were the same as hers. It wasn't nothing at all, but that was what it had to be.

Precious, precious moments. They'd seemed to Sam to last for years. As if caught in Eloise's gaze, he'd been sucked into a vortex where time stood still. As if they'd said all of the things that needed to be said, got to know and trust each other, and found themselves in a place where just this one look was enough to hold everything that a man might feel for a woman. To receive everything that he couldn't help wanting in return.

And, of course, it had to end. They'd been called back and Eloise had clung to his arm on the stairs, in a sweet echo of what had gone before. By the time they reached the Great Hall, where Paul and Aunt Celeste were rearranging chairs so that they could sit in front of the inglenook for coffee, there were two feet of empty air between them.

It seemed that Grant family traditions were much the same as those of the Douglas family and the after-dinner talk drifted to medical matters. Paul had been approached to write a book based on a series of lectures he'd given, and Aunt Celeste had been proofreading the first few chapters for him.

'It would really interest you, Sam. It's about doctor-patient relationships in primary care. Some of the conclusions are applicable to many different kinds of structures where knowledge and trust are involved and it's very readable, even if you're not working in a medical setting,' Aunt Celeste remarked.

'I'll be very keen to get my hands on it.'

Paul smiled an acknowledgement. 'I'll send you the first few chapters if you're interested. I'd very much like to hear your comments.'

'I'll just mention that Sam's story from last

Christmas, about a lady he visited on Christmas Eve, is very applicable to Chapter Two.' Aunt Celeste was trying to make the remark sound casual and failing dismally. Everyone forgave her for her rather obvious networking style, because behind it all she had good intentions and a very clear understanding of medical issues.

'I'll bear that in mind...' Sam smiled at Paul.

'Why not tell us?' Eloise had been silently following the conversation and spoke up suddenly.

Right now, everything seemed to hang on her words, her reactions. They could have been having a conversation about garden spades, and Sam would have assessed it by Eloise's response. Sam gave in to the inevitable and started to recount how he'd responded to an urgent call from an elderly woman patient on Christmas Eve. It had turned out that she needed someone to fix the fairy to the top of her tree because she couldn't reach.

'What did you do?' Eloise's eyes were bright with interest.

Sam shrugged. 'I put the fairy on the tree for her, made some cocoa and we sat down and watched a carol service on TV. I was still on call, but no one needed me, and I'd just be sitting at home otherwise.'

'My nephew the softie,' Aunt Celeste teased him.

'What was I going to do? She was all on her own. And we had a great time. We sat up until midnight and she broke out the chocolate liqueurs and we wished each other Happy Christmas.'

'And did you? Have a happy Christmas?' Eloise asked.

The warmth in her face was driving him crazy with longing. Sam decided not to mention that he'd gone back the next day with mince pies and a present for Mrs Cornelius. It wasn't strictly relevant and he wasn't sure he could take too much more of Eloise's approval.

'The other doctors from the practice are all married with families, so I generally volunteer to cover Christmas Day. In the New Year I arranged for someone from a charity that organises companionship for the elderly to visit her.'

Paul nodded. 'Which was no doubt the best thing you could have done to improve her general health.'

'We'll have to wait and see. But yes, she seemed much happier the last time I saw her.'

The evening was winding down, and Aunt Celeste began to yawn behind her hand. When she and Paul excused themselves, Eloise got to her feet and did the same. Sam decided that he'd better turn in as well, and followed them up the stairs, wishing Eloise a good night as he passed her door, forcing himself to walk to his own room without looking back.

He should get a good night's sleep, but Sam was still wide awake. He took off his jacket and tie, then remembered he'd left the book he'd brought with him downstairs. Feeling the chill of the air in the hallway, he walked as quietly as he could along the creaking floorboards, and down to the sitting room. His attention was drawn to the window and he drew the curtains back, looking at the snow outside with the eyes of a practising doctor, rather than a man who had been foolish enough to see the world as a sparkling place for the last few hours.

The snow must have been a couple of feet deep in places, and if this kept up there would be injuries to deal with tomorrow. Blocked roads, which meant that ambulances and paramedics would be struggling to get to their patients. The hospital would be contending with potential staff shortages and increased demand for its services, and that was very bad news.

Bad news that provided him with a challenge. One that was easier to face than this evening's challenges had been. Sam turned from the window, making for the light switch, but before he reached it something caught his eye and he froze.

She was walking along the gallery, which ran at head height along the far wall of the sitting room and was generally used as a short cut from the main staircase to the back of the house. Eloise had folded a thick, pale-coloured blanket like a shawl and draped it around her shoulders. Underneath, a thin white nightdress foamed around her ankles. Somehow she was managing to avoid every creak in the floorboards as she walked and her footsteps were silent. She seemed almost ghostly in the darkness, unaware that he was below her, staring up at her.

She disappeared, and he broke free of the spell. Sam picked up his book from the coffee table listening for anything that might tell him where she'd gone.

Nothing. He couldn't hear her outside and wondered if she'd gone to the kitchen for a glass of water. He should go back upstairs, but something led him in search of Eloise.

By the time he found her in the Great Hall, led by the light that was coming from the fireplace, the chill in the air was making him shiver. She was sitting inside the inglenook, a candle propped in one of the alcoves, her bare feet stretched out towards the stove.

'Can't sleep?' She looked up at him.

'I came downstairs to fetch my book.' Luckily Sam still had the book in his hand as evidence, and Eloise nodded. 'What are you doing in there?'

'It used to be my thinking place, when I was a kid. Come and give it a try.'

Sam couldn't resist. He ducked into the inglenook, finding that when he was inside there was enough space to stand straight and it was surprisingly roomy. The bricks, once stained by smoke, had been cleaned and there were two polished wooden benches let into the wall, one on either side of the stove. Even though the fire had been banked up for the night, the inglenook was beautifully cosy.

'I can see why you like it. It's really warm in here.'

'Yes, it's like this all winter, even when the fire isn't alight. The bricks take in the heat and you're sheltered from the draughts. That was the original idea of an inglenook, a place for the family to keep warm in winter.'

Sam sat down on the bench opposite Eloise. 'Penny for them?'

CHAPTER SIX

SHE JUST HAD to tell him, didn't she? If this was her thinking place, then it stood to reason that Eloise had some thinking to do, and Sam had asked the obvious question. The answer—that she'd been thinking about him—was a place that she wasn't sure she trusted herself, or Sam, enough to go.

'I'll go first, shall I?' He smiled.

Thank you. Thank you *so* much. Eloise nodded, wondering if his thoughts were the same as hers.

'I've got a confession to make. I know that you probably weren't looking forward much to this weekend. Aunt Celeste told me that there was a lot of unfair gossip and bad feeling when your wedding was cancelled at the last minute.'

For a moment she was powerless to speak. Swallowing the lump in her throat didn't make things any better, because Eloise didn't know what to say.

'You don't pull your punches, do you?'

He nodded, something like warmth in his eyes. Eloise couldn't bring herself to trust it any more.

'To be honest, I've been feeling a bit uncomfortable about it. Knowing and not saying anything.'

Okay. That was…it seemed reasonable. These seemed like the actions of a man who cared about the people around him. Who maybe cared a little bit about her.

'And Celeste warned you…' That was a sentence she really didn't want to finish. Celeste had warned her beloved nephew against having too much to do with her. That was probably fair, but it was something of a disappointment.

He raised his eyebrows in surprise. 'Aunt Celeste gave up warning me about things years ago. She was concerned that someone might say the wrong thing, and wanted me to step in and whisk you away if I saw that anyone was giving you a hard time.'

Eloise hadn't realised how much that might mean to her. She'd told herself that she didn't care what anyone else thought, because Gramps knew what had happened, and he supported her all the way. That the comments, mostly behind her back but some to her face, weren't sticks and stones and they couldn't hurt her. But she saw her hand shake as she wiped tears from her face.

'That's so nice of Celeste. I should thank her.'

'Not right now. Probably not ever. I think her intention was that this was going to be a covert operation. I'd move in and divert your attention while she and Paul executed a pincer movement and took care of the guilty party…'

He was trying to make her smile. When she did, she saw warmth blossom in his eyes. Anyone who thought blue was at the cooler end of the colour spectrum should meet Sam.

'What happens in the inglenook stays in the inglenook, then.'

He nodded, stretching his legs out in front of him towards the remaining heat of the stove. Shadows played around his face from the candle, emphasising the strong line of his jaw.

'The wedding…' They both spoke together and Sam smiled.

'You should go first.'

Eloise took a deep breath, trying to order her thoughts. 'After my wedding fell apart, I went away for two weeks, thinking that by the time I got back everything would have quietened down a bit. I hadn't been answering my phone or looking at my email while I was away, and when I read all of the messages, and realised that everyone was really angry with me, I came up here to see Gramps.'

'Who, no doubt, had something constructive to say.'

'He said that I should talk about it in my own time, and not let anyone else push me into doing so before I was ready...' It had been the first loving thing that anyone had said to her. Gramps had trusted her and believed in her. Eloise felt a tear prick at the side of her eye and brushed it away.

Sam was silent for a moment, his brow furrowed in thought. 'And you're not ready now?'

Eloise shrugged. 'I don't know...' Was this Sam's way of asking what had happened? Was she going to give in to the impulse to gain his approval and tell him, when she'd refused to tell anyone else apart from Gramps?

'My guess is that when you are sure you'll know. I can see why you really needed to hear Paul tell you that other people wanting to know wasn't a good reason for you to talk about it.'

A little shiver of alarm ran down Eloise's

spine. Sam was right, but she couldn't see how he'd come to that conclusion. Maybe she'd been foolish in trusting him, even this far, when she really had no idea what his reaction would be.

'Why would you think that?'

'Because…forgive me if I have this wrong…'

'Forgiven.' She just needed to hear what he thought, whatever that was.

'You've already experienced loss.' Sam was clearly treading carefully, watching for her response. 'Your mother and grandmother, and then your father.'

That was fair. 'Yes. Dad couldn't make it for the wedding, and he stayed out of things afterwards. He said it was all too complicated.'

'Maybe you just needed someone to make it very simple. To put you first, without really needing to know exactly what had happened. That's what families are for, isn't it?'

She hadn't thought about it like that. She'd just been so grateful that Gramps *had* supported her, and Eloise hadn't questioned it. Sometimes another point of view came with twenty-twenty vision.

'You have a point. I've always felt that this is the place I really belong, and I needed to know that I still did.'

Talking to Sam made sense of it, even if it brought no answers. It was still hard to trust him, even if he hadn't done anything to deserve her misgivings. Perhaps trust was one of those things that never quite mended, and Michael's betrayal had broken hers irrevocably.

'Can I ask you something?'

He gave a short, barking laugh, as if he knew that whatever she was about to ask might be confronting. 'I can hardly say *no*, can I?'

'Everyone can always say no.' She waited for his answer and, when it didn't come, Eloise asked her question. 'You seem to understand what a bad break-up is like. How much it hurts.'

He shrugged. 'Yes and no. When my parents broke up it was devastating for the whole family. But that's not really what you were asking, is it. There's a difference between being involved in your parents' break-up and being blamed for your own.'

He was very perceptive. Very honest. He seemed to see straight through her and yet somehow he was still here. Still talking.

'I guess so. It's hurtful, either way.'

'It's always been very important to me to respect my partner's right to do whatever she wants. To let her leave, without standing in her way.' He gave a wry smile. 'I don't want to be like my father.'

'That's a good thing, isn't it?'

'I think so. Sometimes it's hard to find closure when someone ends a relationship without telling you why.'

Eloise caught her breath. Did he think that was what she'd done? They seemed suddenly to be staring at each other from opposite sides of the same bad situation.

'I…my fiancé…ex-fiancé… Michael. He was part of the decision and knew exactly why I left.'

Sam looked up suddenly. Something about the way that he couldn't quite meet her gaze told Eloise that she'd just answered the question he hadn't dared ask. He might be a careful and tactful man, but that wasn't the real reason for his restraint. Sam had been hurt too, and he was as cautious as she was.

'I didn't mean to draw any parallels. That's quite different.'

And yet suddenly she felt that he'd broken their connection. She couldn't find Sam's warmth, or his honesty, any more and whatever he was thinking seemed to be reserved for him alone.

'I just meant…' Eloise shrugged. 'I suppose that *is* what I meant. I want you to know.'

He nodded. 'It matters that he knows. No one else needs to.'

'It sounds as if there's something you don't know.' Maybe she was pushing Sam a little too far, asking him to talk about things he didn't want to talk about. But he seemed to be carrying a burden, and maybe he just wanted to put it down for a while.

'My last break-up was the un-messiest in human history. Even Aunt Celeste missed it and she's got unerring radar for those kinds of things. My ex, Alice, said she wanted to take a break and wouldn't tell me why. That was painful in a lot of ways…'

'I hate to tell you this, but that sounds pretty messy to me. Like an explosion in an enclosed space.'

Sam grinned suddenly. 'Yeah. It felt a bit like that too.'

There was nothing more to say. They had answers but there were no conclusions to be drawn, other than that they both needed to tread very carefully. But this was a place from which she could start to know Sam better, without constantly questioning herself about whether she'd said or done the right thing.

'It's been a good talk. I've appreciated it.'

'Me too. But I think that the wondrous effect of the inglenook has to be taken in small doses at first. This is my first time, remember...'

He stretched his arms, and Eloise felt the same thrill that she always did when she watched Sam move. There was a controlled power in his body that always made her shiver.

'I'll see you in the morning, then.' Eloise didn't move. She'd wait until he was safely upstairs and in his own bedroom, so that there was no opportunity to say *yes* to him if he suggested they spend a little more time together tonight. Now that they'd talked, it seemed less essential to grab at every moment with him, fearing that it might never happen again.

'Yes. Don't stay down here too long. I think tomorrow's going to be a busy day.' He got to his feet, ducking out of the inglenook.

'You still want to work with me tomorrow, then?'

He turned, bending down to give her a spine-tingling smile.

'More than ever.'

The expected call came in early the next morning. Aunt Celeste and Paul were sitting at the kitchen table while Sam made a second round of toast for them all. He'd lain awake just long enough to hear Eloise's quiet footsteps in the corridor as she'd gone back to her room and had then fallen into a deep sleep, which he blamed entirely on the benign power of the inglenook. He'd dreamt of Eloise, but those dreams had been free of the nagging doubts and questions that had been bothering him ever since they'd met.

The instant chemistry between them was still challenging, in the face of all their differences. But he understood those differences a little better now, and Eloise had seemed to understand them too. There was a measure of relief in that, and maybe it would allow them to both concentrate on today's work at the Community Hospital.

'Should I go and wake Eloise?' Aunt Celeste asked, and Paul shook his head.

'She's coming. Just had a shower.'

'You know by the creaks in the floorboards, don't you?' Aunt Celeste smiled at him. 'Goodness only knows how these Tudor people managed anything in the way of intrigue. The floorboards must have given them away every time.'

Sam took note of the information, hiding his smile. No intrigue allowed, even if Eloise did seem to know her way around the creaks.

'They probably didn't creak quite so much

when the house was built.' Paul leaned back in his seat. 'You don't like it?'

'I adore it, darling. Advanced warning of when you try to sneak up behind me...'

Sam's attention was distracted as Eloise walked into the kitchen, carrying an emerald-green hat that matched her sweater. When he smiled, she smiled back.

'How many hats do you have?' This was the third he'd counted in as many days.

'A woman can't have hats?' She shot him a look of good-natured defiance, which sent tingles down his spine. There was something about Eloise's defiance that really turned him on.

'I didn't say that.' He took the hat from her hand, putting it onto her head.

Eloise chuckled, pulling it down over her ears. 'Are we up for the hospital today?'

'Yes, and Paul's called Ted already. He's going to meet us with the motor sled, down by the road.' He handed the plate of toast he'd made for himself to Eloise and she picked a slice up, taking a bite.

'You're really going to wish you had a hat when we get to the sledding part of things...'

Last night's snowfall had been heavy, and even if the roads had been passable they would have had to dig their way to Sam's car. They set out along the driveway, struggling in the deep drifts.

Even that short journey was taxing, and by the time they neared the road Aunt Celeste was doubled over, tired out from lifting her feet in the deep snow. Paul was with her, trying to get her to walk just a few more steps, and she was shaking her head.

'You and Eloise go on ahead… I'll catch up, I just need a few moments.' She straightened a little when Sam came to help.

Eloise slid past him, taking Aunt Celeste's arm. 'We're not going anywhere without you.'

'Darling, that's very kind but…' Aunt Celeste protested, but Eloise was clearly not taking any arguments this morning. Sam wondered if she'd found a way to thank his aunt, for having stood by her.

'Look, it's not so deep up ahead.' Eloise pointed to the tree-lined entrance to the drive. 'Sam and I can move the worst of the snow away while you get your breath back.'

Aunt Celeste was a tough cookie, but she knew another strong woman when she saw her. And she knew that families didn't leave each other behind. She nodded, standing with Paul while Sam and Eloise scooped out a narrow path for her.

Eloise had been so eager to do anything she could to please when Sam had first met her. But her fierce protectiveness in taking Aunt Celeste's arm and walking with her to the end of the drive was different from that. Paul had noticed too, but he said nothing, watching the two of them with a smile.

When they reached the road, Sam could see a bulky motor sled at the bottom of the slope on the other side, and a dark-haired middle-aged man leaning against the side of it. He waved, and Eloise helped Aunt Celeste down the slope, bundling her into the front seat next to Ted.

It was a noisy, and very windy and cold, way to travel, but Ted's route across the undisturbed snow in the fields made short work of the journey. The motor sled drew up outside the hospital, next to the sweep of drive that had been cleared of snow to allow ambulances and cars to enter and leave. Eloise had been holding onto her hat, and now pulled it back down over her ears in a show of determination that was all hers, and made her look like a beguiling elf on a mission. Ted turned in his seat.

'I can wait. It doesn't look as if they've made much of a start on clearing the roads yet, and I might be able to get to places that the ambos can't.'

'What about the farm?' Paul asked.

'It'll be okay. All of the animals are fed and Claire's keeping an eye on things. She'll call if she needs me.'

'In that case, why don't you come inside, and we'll see what's happening?'

Ted produced a chain and padlock from under his seat, and the motor sled was secured to a nearby tree. As they entered the hospital a blast of warm air greeted them, and Paul asked the receptionist to call Joe Parrish and tell them they were here.

It was all well organised. Joe handed Sam and Eloise a pair of scrubs each, and told them they'd be working together in the minor injuries department, which could expect to receive any severity of injury while the routes to the main hospital were blocked. Paul and Aunt Celeste were helping organise and lending their expertise where it was needed. Ted would be found a warm place to sit and some coffee, until the motor sled was needed. From the look of things he wouldn't be waiting long.

'Don't look at the queue...' Eloise joined him in the doorway to the waiting room, which was now crammed with people. He couldn't see who was a patient and who wasn't, and everyone seemed equally impatient to see a doctor.

'Yeah, I was just thinking that.' Sam turned away, following her to the overflow treatment area, which had now been readied for patients. There were triage nurses who would work out who needed to see someone most urgently; he didn't have to make those decisions. His time in A&E when he'd been training told him that he was part of a larger machine now.

They worked alongside each other, just a thin curtain separating them. Sam called to Eloise for help with a patient who had been in a car accident, and had multiple bruises and lacerations, and Eloise asked him to take over when a woman turned up with a young baby, saying that she couldn't get to her own doctor. After four hours of concentrated effort, they had fifteen minutes off to go and get a sandwich and something to drink from the canteen.

'What do you say we look now?' Sam stopped by the door to the waiting room as they walked back together. The flow of patients in the last hour had seemed to ease a little.

'Give me a minute to go hide in a corner.' She grinned at him. 'You can tell me lies if you think I can't take the truth.'

Eloise could take any amount of truth, and even though she hadn't told him everything last night, Sam understood why that was. Now, he was pinning all of his hopes for a friendship on the idea that they could turn their backs on the past, and start again. That felt risky, because new starts involved a great deal of trust. But right now, it seemed to be part of a process of looking forward, and not recklessly disregarding the lessons they'd learned.

He opened the door, looking into the waiting room, while Eloise leaned against the wall, her arms folded as if to emphasise the fact that she really *wasn't* looking.

'Not so bad. About a quarter full, and there's a man in one corner who's actually smiling.'

'Really?'

'Look for yourself...'

Eloise grinned. 'I'll take your word for it.' She looked round as Aunt Celeste hurried across the reception area towards them.

'Things seem to be under control here, so would you both be able to go out with Ted? We've had a call from a pub in Terringford. Someone's broken their leg and the village is completely cut off at the moment. Ted's not sure exactly how close he can get, but he thinks he can make it most of the way.'

Sam looked at Eloise and she nodded. 'Yeah, we'll go.'

'Great, thanks. Paul's sorting out splints and a stretcher, along with basic medical supplies, and Ted will be ready to go in five minutes. You can get a couple of hi-vis vests from the receptionist.' Aunt Celeste obviously had everything under control. 'Wrap up warm…'

CHAPTER SEVEN

THEY WALKED OUT to the motor sled, zipping up their jackets as they went. Sam could see Ted, stowing the medical equipment away under the seats, and soon they were skimming across the fields again, the wind biting at their faces. He'd completely lost any sense of where they were, or what direction they were going in, before they drew up at the side of a small stream, which was almost completely frozen over.

'I reckon this is as far as we can go.' Ted was surveying a small footbridge to their left. 'I can't get the sled up onto that bridge.'

'Where are we headed?' Sam asked, and Ted pointed to a cluster of buildings, about half a mile away. 'Right there. But the land dips in between here and there, and it looks as if the snow's drifted. Might be two or three feet deep in places. I can try going around by the road, but it's a fair way and it's generally easier keeping to the fields because there are fewer obstructions.'

'Seems as if it's going to be quicker to walk. What do you think, Sam?' Eloise asked.

'I'll take your word for it. You know the area better than I do. What's that, over there?' There seemed to be a caterpillar trail of people, heading through the snow towards them.

Eloise looked across at them, shading her eyes from the glare of the low sun. 'I think they're digging. If the guy we're going to see needs to go to the hospital, and the sled can't get to him, then we're going to have to get him to the sled.'

Ted nodded. 'When you get there, let them know I'll be on the other side of the footbridge. If they know of a way to get closer, give me a call, but I don't want to risk getting stuck somewhere.'

'Okay, will do. Shall we leave the stretcher here, or do you want to take it with us, Sam?'

'Let's leave it here and just take the medical bag. No point in carrying too much through the snow now if we can send someone back to get the stretcher when there's a path dug.'

They walked across the footbridge, sliding down the icy sheet that covered it on the far side. Once they were on solid ground, the first few hundred yards weren't too bad, but suddenly Eloise took a step and sunk down into the loose, powdery snow.

'Oh! Stay over that side, Sam, it's deep here.' The snow was already up to her knees, and she was still sinking gently. A shout echoed across from the men who were digging, and Sam saw two of them gesturing to keep to the left, where he'd been walking.

'Great. Telling us that a bit sooner might have been useful.' She raised her voice, yelling back to the men. 'Doctors!'

'Go that way!' one of the men yelled back, gesturing again to their left.

'Right then. We'll go left, shall we?' Eloise rolled her eyes, and Sam couldn't help smiling.

She pulled her hat down over her ears in a now familiar gesture. She'd sunk a bit further now, and was struggling to get out of the snow. Sam took a step towards her, and she waved him back.

'You're heavier than me so you'll sink faster.' She looked around, her gaze coming to rest on the bag he was carrying. 'How about detaching the strap and just sliding it over to me? I think I just need something to hang on to. I'm not stuck but I can't get any leverage.'

Sam bent down, unclipping the strap. Winding one end around his arm, he spun the other end across the surface of the snow towards her. Eloise reached out, catching hold of it.

'Got it? I'm going to try and pull you out. Tell me if you want me to stop.'

'Okay. Now's really good. I'm still sinking.'

As Sam pulled, Eloise dropped onto her stomach. Her legs slid out of the snow easily and she scrambled towards him. He hoped that she wasn't too wet, but she got to her feet seeming ready to press on.

'Thanks.' She was brushing snow off her jacket and waterproof trousers. 'I'm not going to do that again. It was no fun at all.'

It was hard going, and Sam could feel moisture seeping over the tops of his boots, but they made it. Eloise stopped for a moment to ask the men who were digging if there was a better way around for the Skidoo, and one of them shook his head.

'No, the road's pretty narrow, and it's partly blocked by a couple of abandoned cars. A one-seater sled could make it, but Ted's is too wide.'

'You're going to keep digging then? We're going to need to get our patient over to the sled.'

'Yeah, we've got more people coming. We'll get there.'

'Great. Thanks.'

Eloise's practicality and easy manner seemed to allow her an entrée into this rural community where everyone knew everyone else. It was easy to trust her professionally, and Sam was working less and less hard to trust her personally now. The group of men stood back to let them through and they hurried along the pathway that had already been dug from the back door of the pub. When they entered the main bar, it was empty.

'Hello! Doctors!' Eloise called out and a voice sounded from the other bar.

'Through here...'

The man was lying on one of the long upholstered benches, in a smaller snug bar. His shoe and sock had already been removed, and his trouser leg cut. From the look of his leg it was probably broken. A man and woman were with him and the man stepped forward to greet them.

'This is my pub. Kevin's taken a fall, and we brought him in here.'

'Where did he fall—outside in the snow?'

'No, he fell down the steps to the basement. I got the lads to carry him back up here and we made him as comfortable as we could.'

Understandable, but maybe not the best thing to do in the circumstances. Sam guessed she would have preferred to have seen the leg kept immobile as long as there were no immediate dangers in keeping Kevin where he was, but Eloise didn't press the point. Her disciplined use of her time was obvious—she gave no impression of rushing, but her questions were all to the point and about things that they needed to know.

'All right. One of our priorities is to find a way of getting him safely to the motor sled, so if you can find a few more volunteers to help the men who are already digging that would be great.'

She turned to Kevin, kneeling down beside him. 'Hi Kevin, I'm Eloise and this is Sam, we're both doctors. Just for the avoidance of any doubt, I can see that your leg must be hurting, but is there anywhere else that you feel pain?'

'No.'

'Good. Bump your head? What about your back—did you land on the base of your spine?'

She was calm and assured, getting as much information as she could in the shortest possible time. It was a little different from Sam's work—he might not always have as much time as he wanted to spend with his patients, but he had access to their records and could assess them in that context. Eloise was starting from scratch, and she was clearly very good at setting people at ease and inspiring confidence. Sam was confident enough in her to take a back seat role.

'All right, here's the one you've been waiting for. How much pain do you feel on a score of one to ten? One, you're feeling pretty good, and ten's the most pain you've ever felt.'

'Um… Don't know. Seven? And a half, probably.'

'Seven and a half. Ever broken a bone before?'

Kevin shook his head. 'I had appendicitis when I was a kid. I think that might have been a ten.'

'Ever had an allergic reaction before?'

'Feathers. They make me sneeze.'

'Oh. Okay. Hear that, Sam? No feathers.'

'Gotcha.'

Eloise left Sam to administer the analgesic and carry on with some basic checks, while she took a pad from her pocket, writing down the time and the details that Sam was calling out as he went. She was rubbing her leg and suddenly put the pad down, stripping off her waterproof trousers. Underneath there was a wet patch on one side of her jeans, which must be so cold by now that it hurt. Sam reached for the pad and Eloise went to stand by the radiator, rubbing her leg.

'Resting heart rate sixty beats a minute.' She was back and smiling as if nothing had happened. 'That's perfect, Kevin.'

Kevin grinned. 'I like to keep myself in shape. I do gym work twice a week.'

'Great. I'm afraid you might have to give that a rest for a while, but make sure you get back to it when you can. How old are you?'

'Twenty-two.'

'Got a girlfriend?' That meant that the next part of this was going to hurt.

'Nah.'

'Waiting for the right one to come along, eh?'

Kevin grinned suddenly. 'Yeah. There's someone I like, a girl at the gym. We go for coffee.'

Eloise nodded. 'Just getting to know her, then. It's nice to have someone who shares your interests, isn't it. This next part's going to hurt a bit, but we'll be as quick as we can. Just hang on in there, eh?'

She'd planted the idea of the girl that Kevin liked in his head. Maybe he'd be a little braver for her, and maybe for Eloise. At this moment, Sam would have walked across hot coals for her.

Eloise examined the leg, stopping when Kevin cried out. 'Sorry about that. We're all good, nearly done.'

She was quick but careful. Kevin began to shift a little and Sam urged him to stay still, while Eloise kept going.

'All done.' She gave the lad a dazzling smile. 'You did great, and you can rest a bit now. Take a few deep breaths. Your leg's broken, as we thought, and we'll be putting a temporary splint on it, which will make you much more comfortable. Then we'll take you to the hospital. That's going to be a ride on a motor sled, I'm afraid, but we'll have you well strapped in and it won't take very long.'

'Ted's motor sled?' Kevin asked. 'I asked him if I could go for a ride on it once and he told me to sling my hook.'

'Well, he won't be doing that today. This one's all about getting you where you need to go.'

'Cool. Don't suppose I can drive it, can I...?'

'No, Kevin. I don't suppose you can. Particularly after the injection that Sam's just given you. How's it feeling now?'

'Better. More comfortable.'

She sorted through the bag, finding the splint that she wanted. Then she turned to

Sam, murmuring quietly, 'It's definitely broken, I felt it move. Thankfully, carrying him up here doesn't seem to have made it any worse and I don't think it's misaligned. We'll have to be very careful when we put the leg into the splint, though. I'll lift it and you slip the splint underneath?'

'Yep. That's good.'

She turned to Kevin again. 'Nearly there now…'

When Sam walked out of the pub, he found that the village had been busy. Men, women, and even a few children were digging, and the path through the snow almost reached the Skidoo. He called Ted, asking him to get someone to bring the stretcher down and turned just as a snowball whizzed through the air, hitting him on the shoulder.

'Gotcha!' Eloise was almost doubled up with laughter, and Sam couldn't help but smile. Working seemed to bring out a sense of fun in her, an assurance, which made her even more difficult to resist.

'Not fair. Where's my warning?' He bent down, gathering up a handful of snow, but he was too slow. Eloise had ducked back into the doorway before he could pack the loose snow together. But as he drop-kicked the snowball into a shower of small pieces she popped back out again.

'Grants don't play fair, Sam. Didn't you know?'

Eloise was exhausted and aching by the time they got home. She'd spend half the afternoon in wet jeans, which had only dried out after they'd reached the warmth of the hospital, and she'd taken Kevin into the temporary A&E department to arrange for X-rays on his leg, before going back to work alongside Sam for another couple of hours.

Ted had already taken Gramps and Celeste home, and he returned just as it started to snow again, taking them back over fields that shone in the moonlight. As soon as the front door had closed behind them, Celeste hurried out of the kitchen, stripping them of their coats and shooing them into the sitting room. They flopped down at opposite ends of the long sofa, too tired to even speak.

'How do you think the party's going so far?' Sam was leaning back, staring at the ceiling, his feet stretched out towards the fire.

'Good. Perhaps we should do next Christmas in A&E.' Actually, Eloise had done last Christmas in A&E. Not with Sam, though.

'Too much. We should save this kind of celebration for the really big events.'

'You've got a point. We'll see if we can book the kid who tried to bite me. He really made my evening.'

Sam turned his head towards her. 'Somebody tried to bite you? Did he break the skin?'

'No, but he had fantastic muscle tone in his jaw. Didn't you hear me yowling on the other side of the curtain?'

'Come to think of it, yes, I do recall it. I thought you were torturing Kevin again.'

'No, Kevin and I are cool. He asked me if I wanted to go for coffee with him.'

Sam's grin surfaced suddenly and he put his hand to his heart in a gesture of mock dismay. 'You were going to go for coffee without me? I'm devastated.'

Eloise laughed. 'Don't be jealous. I told Kevin that coffee assignations are special and that he should keep them for the young lady he likes at the gym.'

As soon as the words had left her lips, Eloise knew she'd said the wrong thing. The humour died in his eyes, and he wiped his hand across his face.

'I'm not jealous. I'm sorry if it came across that way. You can go for coffee with whoever you like.'

Actually, she couldn't and Sam knew that just as well as she did. A twenty-two-year-old patient, with enough analgesics in his system to be legally intoxicated, was way off-limits. But that wasn't really the point. Sam had spent much of his childhood watching his father trying to coerce his mother back into a relationship. He'd seen controlling behaviour and probably jealousy and he'd rejected that in his own life, to the point that he felt he had to apologise if a little harmless flirting went in the wrong direction.

And Sam was the last person who should feel that way. He was a kind man, who'd shown her nothing but respect. She'd made a mistake and this was one that she could own.

'Sam, I guess you might know what real jealousy looks like, and I shouldn't have joked about it. I didn't think and it's you that deserves an apology, not me. I'm really sorry.'

'Don't…' He stopped himself, starting again. 'Actually, I really appreciate you saying that. My father was a very jealous man, and it's a bit of a sore point.'

There was more to say. But no need to say it right now, because Sam had reached out, propping his arm on the cushions at the back of the sofa. When Eloise did the same their fingertips barely touched, but the contact meant everything. They'd broken through one piece of the barrier that separated them.

'Eloise… Sam…' Celeste's voice drifted through from the kitchen. 'Dinner's ready!'

Sam smiled, shaking his head at his aunt's timing. He leaned forward and when he brushed a kiss against her cheek Eloise felt exhilaration run through her veins like fire. She'd made no mistake—Sam felt just the same as she did. But whatever they decided to do about it was going to have to wait.

CHAPTER EIGHT

IT HAD BEEN a good evening, not a great evening, and Sam had been left with an inevitable feeling of unfinished business. After a leisurely meal, followed by an hour around the kitchen table talking, Paul had gone up to Eloise's bedroom with her to investigate why the radiator wasn't giving out any heat. Aunt Celeste had gathered up her book and her glasses and made for her bedroom, and Sam had had little option but to go to his.

That was okay. It was hard to leave the smouldering glances that had passed between him and Eloise behind for the night, but they had an understanding now. Their relationship might turn into any one of a thousand different things but, whatever came next, they could be honest with each other.

The following morning, Ted met them by the main road again and dropped them off at the hospital, leaving them to join other farmers in helping to clear the roads that led to villages that had been cut off. The local council was clearing the major roads, and by tomorrow they should be able to make the journey by car. But the Community Hospital was still under pressure, struggling to reach everyone who was already under their care and to deal with the flood of injuries that had been caused by the icy weather conditions.

They'd worked for three hours and the crowd in the waiting room was beginning to thin out a little. Just as Sam was wondering whether they might be able to take ten minutes for coffee, Aunt Celeste came hurrying into the treatment area.

'Eloise, Sam… We have a patient coming in, from one of the houses that's just a little way along the road. There's an ambulance team there now, and he's had a myocardial infarction. Can you get ready to receive him?'

'There's no way of getting him across to the main hospital?' Eloise frowned. The treatment room was well equipped, but Sam knew that it wasn't the best place for emergency cases like this.

'It'll take far too long by road, even if they can make it. We've put a call in for the air ambulance, but they're very busy and it may be anything up to an hour before they can get to us.'

Eloise nodded. 'What facilities do we have here? I know there's a defibrillator, and an ECG. Do we have an echocardiogram?'

'Yes, and the sonographer is on her way down. Blood tests can obviously be taken here, but they're sent over to the lab in the main hospital.'

Eloise puffed out a breath. 'Okay, so no results for any blood tests we do. We'll take the patient's history, diagnose and medicate, and…hope that what we have here is enough.'

It wasn't an ideal situation by any stretch of the imagination. Eloise was used to having the resources of a large hospital at her disposal, and she was obviously frustrated. But when the ambulance crew arrived, she turned to their patient with a bright smile on her face. Sam was relieved to see that he was conscious and even managed to return her smile.

'Hello there. My name's Eloise and I'm a doctor. You're Terry… Sixty-two years old… Do you have anyone with you, Terry?'

'No, I called my brother and his wife when I first started to feel ill but they can't get here.'

'Yeah, this snow's making getting around difficult isn't it.' Eloise was flipping through the notes that the ambulance crew had left.

'Don't you worry, we'll be taking good care of you and if you give me your brother's number I'll make sure he knows what's going on. You're having pain in your chest and upper arm, and you feel sick and breathless.'

'Yes, Doctor. Am I going to the main hospital?'

'We're getting some transport arranged for you right now, just in case you need it. But we'll be treating you here for the time being.' Eloise gave Terry another bright smile, as if nothing was bothering her about the arrangement. It was important to keep heart patients as calm as possible, and Sam reckoned her smile was better than any sedative.

'Okay, I need…' Eloise turned and found that there was no nurse standing behind her waiting for instructions. 'I'll go and get some medication to make you feel more comfortable and my colleague will be taking good care of you in the meantime.'

She turned to Sam, the smile falling from her face to leave an intent look. 'Could you see what you can get in the way of history, do another ECG, and get the echocardiogram started whenever it arrives?'

Sam nodded. Turning to Terry, he introduced himself and started to go through the list of questions that needed to be asked.

* * *

Half an hour later, Terry had been given blood thinners and analgesics to alleviate the pain in his chest, and Eloise had co-opted one of the nurses to sit with him and administer oxygen when it was needed. There were ECGs from the ambulance crew, and after he'd arrived here, tucked into his notes, and Sam had managed to get hold of his GP to get a full history. The sonographer was carrying out an echocardiogram when Paul arrived, wanting an update.

'From the look of the ECG, it's an NSTEMI.' Eloise and Sam had stepped away from Terry's bedside and Eloise handed the ECG printout to Paul. 'See, there's a T wave inversion with no progression to the Q wave.'

That was relatively good news. An NSTEMI was a partial blockage of the coronary artery, and less serious than a full blockage, although it was still considered a medical emergency.

Paul nodded. 'Okay, I've been on to the air ambulance and they'll be another half an hour. Can you keep him stable?'

'We're going to have to. His medical history isn't very encouraging, hypertension and high cholesterol, and there's a family history of heart disease. He doesn't take much exercise and he's a little overweight.'

'Has his GP addressed any of this?' Paul looked at Sam.

'She said that she's been trying.' Sam hadn't been much impressed with the GP's monitoring of Terry's health, but knew from experience that any doctor relied on patients turning up for appointments and doing as they were asked. 'I've made a note, and hopefully the hospital can get to the root of the problem and make sure that the situation's resolved.'

'I'll speak to one of my contacts over there and see what she can do.'

'Is there anyone in the medical profession you *don't* know, Gramps? If so I'll hunt them down and introduce them to you.'

Paul shot her an amused look. 'It gets things done, Eloise. I'm sure that Sam would agree with me.'

Sam held up his hands in a gesture of surrender. 'Don't involve me in this. Particularly since I'm not sure whether this is a professional or family disagreement.'

'Bit of both probably.' Eloise shrugged. 'And it would be great if you *could* get someone to find out what's happening and address the issue, Gramps.'

'My pleasure—' Paul smiled at her '—Dr Grant.'

Eloise was trying not to show it, but she

was worried. She'd done every test that she could, and had written a very full set of notes. Terry was responding to medication and when the air ambulance arrived he was in a stable condition. But as Sam was seeing his next patient off she popped her head around the curtain that separated them, suddenly all smiles. The consultant she'd been speaking to at the main hospital had called to say that Terry had arrived, and thanked her for her thorough work in a difficult situation.

'It's made me realise how lucky I am to work in a large hospital where everything's on site. How on earth do you coordinate everything, Sam?'

'I have contacts...' Sam chuckled as she shot him a look that could have sliced through concrete. 'Are you ready for lunch?'

'Ten minutes. I've just got to finish up with a dislocated finger...'

The small cafeteria was bursting with people, and Eloise made a beeline for a table that had just become empty, leaving Sam in the queue still with their sandwiches and drinks. When he squeezed past busy tables, avoiding coats that had slipped onto the floor, she was sitting staring at a local paper that someone had left behind on the table.

'What's that?' Whatever it was, it appeared that it was far more interesting than the sandwich and coffee that Eloise had raced here to get.

She lowered the paper. When Sam tried to take it from her she held onto it and he had to give it a little tug before she'd let go.

It was actually a very nice picture—Eloise and him, outside the Grand Elk pub yesterday, her arm curved still from throwing a snowball, and his raised to shield himself. Sam assumed that it was the headline that had prompted the annoyed look on Eloise's face.

Doctors in snowball fight outside Grand Elk pub, where man lies injured!

His first thought was to shrug it off, the way he always did with anything that angered him. Sam's second thought was to get in touch with the paper and ask for a copy of the photograph, because it had caught Eloise's smile and the joyous way that she'd moved when she'd taken one moment to break the pressure of the afternoon. Neither of those were going to help.

'That's not the whole story, is it?'

'No, but it's what everyone's going to think.'

And what everyone thought had already

hurt her. Sam considered what Eloise's next course of action might be, and somehow the anger and hurt didn't seem quite so inappropriate when he felt it on her behalf.

'We're not going to apologise for this.'

'We? I'm the one throwing the snowball.'

'I'm sure that's a smile on my face, isn't it?' Sam squinted at the picture. The resolution of the image didn't make it easy to see, but he remembered smiling.

He scanned the short article. It briefly alluded to a man having been taken to hospital, and then added insult to injury by asking readers to send in their own pictures of people taking time off to enjoy the snow.

'It's just annoying. There are people here working really hard, staying overnight away from their families so that they can keep the place running. And they don't even mention that. They pick a picture of me horsing around in the snow.'

'That's not your fault. The paper's misrepresented things.' A thought occurred to him. 'Do you suppose that Joe Parrish has seen this? He might issue a statement.'

'And say what? He wasn't there, and the camera doesn't lie.'

In this instance it had. 'Can you do something for me? Let me sort this out.'

Eloise shook her head, taking the paper from him and folding it in half, then throwing it onto the seat beside her. 'Let it go, Sam. It's irritating, but it doesn't really matter. Let's just rise above it.'

All the things he'd risen above, over the years. His father's behaviour, the way that Alice had left him. He'd be giddy from altitude sickness before too long…

'Okay. We'll rise above it. Will you give me your permission to say what I think, though?'

He saw the look in her eyes soften as she smiled. 'Always say what you think, Sam.'

A shiver ran down his spine. That sounded a lot like trust.

'You're sure?'

'Eat first.' She pointed to his sandwich. 'And drink. We're back on duty in half an hour.'

Part one of his plan was to call Aunt Celeste, and get her to mention the article to Joe. Sam had no doubt that her talent for convincing everyone of her own point of view would ensure that Eloise wasn't questioned about the article.

Part two had been slightly more difficult. But the application of a little judicious outrage while chatting to one of the nurses did the trick. By mid-afternoon, pretty much everyone that they were working with was talking about the 'nonsense' in the paper, and he even heard one of Eloise's patients telling her how unfair it all was, particularly since she was a volunteer.

'What are you doing, Sam?' She popped her head around the curtain as soon as she'd dealt with the man. 'This isn't a propaganda war, you know.'

'I just mentioned it in passing.' He gave her an innocent look.

Suddenly she smiled. It was like the sun breaking through clouds on a rainy day, and Sam couldn't help smiling back.

'What am I going to do with you, Sam?'

Anything she liked. He resisted the temptation to tell her so. 'Doesn't the Grant family stick up for their team?'

'Not all of them. It appears the Douglas family is currently running rings around us on that score.' She gave him a wry smile, disappearing back behind the curtain.

Eloise felt it, even if she chose to dismiss it. And if Sam was going a little over the top about defending her on this, then maybe it was because he could do nothing about the other issues she'd faced with her extended family.

He couldn't do anything about the issues

he'd faced with his father either. Or the way he felt he had to measure every one of his actions against that, striving to be different. But this he could do something about. And now he'd made his mind up, he wouldn't let Eloise down.

Sam turned to the woman who was being shown to his cubicle by one of the volunteers. She was cradling her arm and he could see bruises and swelling around her wrist. Another fall, if he wasn't much mistaken.

'Hello, I'm Sam and I'm a doctor. Sorry you've had to wait so long...'

'Where did Sam go?' Eloise met up with Gramps and Celeste a couple of hours after her shift was supposed to have finished. They'd worked through the backlog of patients, and the night staff seemed to have everything under control. Sam had been right there with her, and then suddenly he hadn't. She'd looked for him but couldn't find him anywhere.

'He'll be along later.' Gramps propelled her out of the hospital, waving to Ted, who had just drawn up in the motor sled.

'How's he going to be along later, if we leave him behind?' Eloise had an idea that Sam was off somewhere, trying to correct a newspaper article that was annoying but in the scheme of things really didn't matter so much. She felt a little guilty about that, because he really should be on his way home for something to eat.

'He'll manage.' Celeste seemed to have some inkling of what was going on and put her arm around Eloise's shoulders, perhaps for comfort and maybe just to make sure she didn't escape and go to find Sam. 'And there's no point in trying to stop him. Sam gets it into his head to do something, and he does it.'

Eloise wondered how Celeste would take it if she mentioned that Sam had said much the same about his aunt. Probably not badly—they seemed close enough to have made that clear already.

'I heard you mentioned that newspaper article to Joe Parrish. I really appreciate it...' There was no need, but it meant a lot that Celeste had stood up for her like that.

'I told him the truth, that's all.' Even so, Celeste looked pleased that Eloise mentioned it. 'I don't like it when people are given a hard time for something they didn't do.'

'Well, strictly speaking, I did do it...'

'Oh, you Grants, you're so literal about things!' Celeste shot her a grimace. 'I saw the article and the clear implication was that you and Sam were messing around all day and ignoring people who needed you. That's not fair, is it, Paul?'

Gramps chuckled. 'No, darling.'

'Don't you *no darling* me, as if you're just agreeing in order to keep the peace, Paul.' Celeste smiled up at Gramps.

'No, my sweet. I've already told you what I think about it. Weren't you listening…?'

The two of them walked to the motor sled, teasing each other amiably. They made Eloise feel around a thousand years old sometimes, seemingly free of the burdens that life brought and madly in love with each other. There was no way that Eloise could ever see herself doing that again, however much she wanted to when she felt the warmth of Sam's gaze.

But Sam and his gaze were nowhere in evidence. Eloise sat in the kitchen, playing with her food for a while, and when Celeste decided to have an early night and finish her book off in bed, Gramps said he'd join her. Eloise hovered by the window, watching as it began to snow again outside.

Then she saw him, a dark figure trudging along the drive, his hat pulled down around his ears and his hands in his pockets. She resisted the impulse to run to the door for a full thirty seconds, and then walked out into the hallway, opening the front door to find Sam kicking the snow off his boots in the porch.

'You must be freezing!' Not the way she really wanted to greet him. A kiss to welcome him home would have been better.

He grinned at her. 'It's chilly out there. Just started snowing again.'

'How far have you walked?' That wasn't the way she wanted to greet him either.

'I got a lift most of the way.' He took off his gloves and coat, rubbing his hands together to warm them.

'Come and warm up. I'll heat some soup for you and there's half a shepherd's pie in the fridge.' Eloise chivvied him into the kitchen, moving him out of the way of the cast iron range cooker so she could heat the soup. He was standing close, leaning against the oven as if gravitating towards the heat.

'Any other questions?'

'No. But whatever you've done, you didn't really need to…'

She'd said the wrong thing. Eloise had meant it as a thank-you for going that extra mile for her, doing more than was necessary in defending her. But Sam suddenly stiffened, walking over to the other side of the kitchen to stare out of the window. Suddenly the room felt very cold.

It was impossible to let this go, and just leave things as they were. If explaining made everything worse, then so be it. Eloise followed him, nudging him gently to get his attention, which seemed to be focused on the falling snow outside.

'I meant that you didn't need to do whatever it is you've done, but I really appreciate that you walked that extra mile for me. Particularly since you were walking it in the snow…'

The ghost of a smile flickered on his face. 'Even if I was fuming all the way?'

Sam had an issue with anger. Through all of the ups and downs of the weekend, this was the first time she'd heard him express even the slightest exasperation with anything, and she could understand why. His father must have been an angry man.

'Being indignant on my behalf makes me like it even better. Just as long as you weren't *too* indignant with the newspaper people.'

His eyebrows shot up, and the look on his face was almost one of guilt. 'Did Aunt Celeste tell you?'

'No, your secret was safe with her. But it's not much of a leap. You weren't at the hospital when we left and the newspaper's office isn't too far from there.'

She heard the soup begin to bubble ferociously. Eloise grabbed his hand, not willing to end this conversation just yet, and Sam followed her across the room. She pulled the pot off the hotplate, turning her attention back on him.

'So did you pound on their door, demanding to be let in?'

He was smiling now. 'No, I gave them a call and asked if anyone was in the office, because I wanted to drop in and correct an error. I had coffee with a young man whose job description seems to be dealing with whatever happens after six o'clock.'

'And you didn't put snow down the back of his neck?' She could tease him a little now.

'No, I didn't. I may have felt like doing so when I arrived...'

'That's okay. As long as you didn't actually do it. And I really do appreciate you having gone to such lengths for me.'

'Even if you don't need it?'

'It's the thought that counts and I reckon I needed that. I *was* considering apologising but... I think I may be done with saying sorry. Unless I actually am sorry, that is.'

He gave a smiling nod. 'That's not a bad idea. You don't have anything to be sorry for.'

'Not for the snowball. For the other thing.'

'You mean calling a halt to your marriage? Can I ask you something?'

'Go ahead.' Eloise almost wished that he would insist on knowing what had happened. It would be an end to all of her conflicting feelings about telling him. But Sam had told her she didn't need to explain, and that had been the end of it.

'Did you love him?'

'When I said I'd marry him I did. When I left I wasn't sure, but what I did know was that I had no respect for him.'

'And now?'

'No. Not even a little bit.' How could she? Michael had taken his revenge on her, letting everyone turn up at the church when he knew full well that she wasn't going to be there. When *he'd* told her to go.

'That's all that matters then. If you don't love him then you don't need another reason.'

'How do you leave these things behind? Do you know, Sam?' He'd been hurt too.

'If I did, I'd tell you. I don't.'

'Too bad.' She turned her mouth down. 'I was hoping there might be a magic formula.'

Maybe her magic formula was standing

right here, and she just didn't see. She didn't need someone to forgive her, because the only forgiveness that really mattered was the one that she could find for herself. She needed someone that she could trust, and Eloise could see herself trusting Sam. In a sudden impulse she shifted against him, winding her arms around his neck.

That burning gaze of his. She could get lost in it, feeling its warmth sear her. At this moment, there was nothing she wouldn't do to have him close.

She felt Sam's arms tighten around her, and the hard strength of his body against hers. His lips touched hers, holding back to make the moment last, in an exquisite blend of longing and temptation.

And then tenderness gave way to passion and he kissed her. Eloise felt Sam's body move against her, saw the way his eyes darkened suddenly, and she knew that he was all hers.

'We can't do this, Sam. Not even if we really want to.' There might be a time when she could trust him, even one where she could trust herself. But the future wasn't here yet. Maybe it wouldn't ever be.

'Yeah, I know. But you make me believe it's possible, Eloise.'

'You make me believe it too.'

'Then...could we try it one more time? Just one more kiss?'

'Because staying in this beautiful house, being snowed in together is so romantic?' Eloise wasn't entirely sure that she wanted Sam to sweep her off her feet like this. It was what Michael had done, using the charm that he'd later used against her.

'No, I want you to know exactly what you're doing. Kissing me in a cold kitchen, when we're both tired from a day's work.'

What Sam wanted seemed far more romantic than anything that Michael could have dreamed up. Two cool heads and the commonplace, turned into magic by being together.

'Another kiss would be my pleasure, Sam...'

CHAPTER NINE

IT HAD BEEN hard to go to his room alone. Not having any condoms to hand wouldn't have been a deal-breaker, because Sam was sure that they could still find things to do together. But he wasn't going to think about that. Wanting Eloise was terrifying, because he'd never wanted a woman as much, and certainly never after having known her for such a short time. It was the kind of sure knowledge that nothing would be right until they were together that he'd seen in his father's actions.

Sam had woken before dawn, looking out of the window to find that another couple of inches of snow had fallen. That wouldn't be enough to block the roads that were already open, but the conditions would be icy. He got dressed, hoping that the creak of the stairs wouldn't wake everyone up, and slipped out of the house.

He'd roughly cleared almost half of the

driveway when Eloise appeared, her arms wrapped around her as she ran towards him, the thick sweater she was wearing obviously doing nothing to keep her warm.

'Brr... It's cold this morning. Come inside. I've made you some breakfast.'

Sam didn't need to be asked twice. A little exercise, to work off the nerves about whether his conversation at the newspaper office was going to come to anything, had seemed like a good idea, but now he was getting cold and tired. He followed Eloise inside, knocking the snow from his boots before seeking the warmth of the kitchen.

Paul and Aunt Celeste were already up, and there was a place set for him at the table. Eloise set a plate down in front of him, containing bacon, eggs and tomatoes with a pile of hash browns.

'That's just what I need. Thank you.' Sam noticed that Eloise's tablet was lying on the table.

'It's there. I've seen it.' Eloise was grinning at him, and he realised that she was one step ahead of him.

'I didn't tell Eloise to look.' Aunt Celeste was keen to protest her innocence. 'But you can't stop an intelligent woman from working things out. It goes against the grain.'

He nodded, starting to tuck into his breakfast. 'All right. So what did it say?'

'It's a lovely piece.' She sat down opposite him, beaming. 'Right at the top of their news pages on the web.'

'It's called *"We'd like to set the record straight"*,' Aunt Celeste added approvingly. 'It'll be published in next week's paper as well.'

'Good. I'm going to finish my breakfast and read it through. Just to make sure they put in everything I asked them to.'

Eloise winced. 'You had a list?'

'Aide memoire.'

No one looked particularly convinced of that. But Sam didn't want to share any more. If he couldn't go back and put the past right, then maybe he had some say over the future. Last night, when he'd held Eloise close and kissed her and she'd kissed him back, he'd seen a tantalising possibility of what that future might be.

But right now he had to stop thinking about that. When breakfast was finished, they left Aunt Celeste and Paul to clear away and he and Eloise went out to finish clearing the drive. That, and working alongside her at the Community Hospital, was the kind of sharing that was real and able to provide solid foundations of trust that they could build on.

At lunchtime the stream of patients began to dry up, and they had a whole hour's break. Sam was looking forward to spending the time sitting with Eloise and drinking coffee when one of the other volunteers, a nurse who had left her two small children with her husband to go back and help at the hospital, came up with a better idea. Lottie's mischievous sense of humour had kept them all going when it seemed that they'd never cope. And her announcements in the waiting room had become legendary, making patients feel that they were part of a group effort with their doctors, and that they would all be seen in order, even if there was a long wait.

'Snowball fight!'

Eloise clapped her hand across her mouth, almost dancing with glee. 'That's so wrong…!'

'Yes, isn't it. Whatever would the papers say?'

'I could call them and let them know…' Sam took his phone from his pocket.

'No! They have to track the story down for themselves, Sam.' Eloise was laughing. 'There's no fun in it if they don't.'

Paul and Aunt Celeste had caught wind of

the enterprise and trooped out with them onto the open land behind the hospital.

'Douglas versus Grant, eh?' Aunt Eloise took Sam's arm. 'I'm claiming the best throwing arm.'

'Oh, really?' Eloise pulled a face of mock outrage. 'Watch out for your nose, Sam…'

He chuckled, covering his nose with his hand, and Aunt Eloise gave Paul a very sportsmanlike hug before he was sent off to join Eloise and the other three people on their team.

'Right now, Sam, I can't throw as well as you, particularly since I had that frozen shoulder. So I'll keep you going with snowballs, and you just keep throwing.'

Sam raised his eyebrows. 'Don't you think that you should exercise the shoulder a bit?'

'Well, of course, and I do.' Aunt Celeste rolled her eyes. 'But we're talking about family honour.'

'You should have thought about that when you went and got engaged to a Grant.' Sam grinned at her.

'Nonsense. Paul and I fight all the time, we both rather like it. *You* might think about it, Sam…'

Had Aunt Celeste's knowing eye seen what was happening between him and Eloise? It was just as well that she hadn't asked outright, because Sam had no way of explaining it, or how he felt about it. But right now that didn't matter, because Eloise and Paul were lobbing snowballs in their direction, and Aunt Celeste had already dodged a particularly well aimed one. After the stress and hard work of the last couple of days, this was fun.

At two o'clock the doctors in the temporary A&E department started to compete for patients. Then at three the announcement came. The hospital was enormously grateful for everything that the volunteers had done in helping to keep things going. Now that the roads were open again, and the main hospital was accessible to ambulances and patients, they should go home, secure in the knowledge that they'd done a fantastic job.

Paul seemed restless, energised by the early mornings and the gruelling workload. Sam could identify with that, they'd been doctors with a mission that had suddenly been whipped out from under them. He couldn't regret that there were no patients left to treat, but adrenaline was still buzzing in his veins.

'What about the pictures?' Paul nudged Aunt Celeste. 'That film we wanted to see is still on.'

'Is it? That's a good idea, we really shouldn't miss it. How do you both feel about subtitles?' Aunt Celeste turned to Sam and Eloise.

'Um….' Eloise looked up at Sam. She clearly felt the same as he did, that Paul and Aunt Celeste's taste in films was great, but that she wanted something that didn't require sitting still for two hours.

'Perhaps we'll give that one a miss. Catch it later in London.' Sam ignored the knowing look that passed between Aunt Celeste and Paul. Whatever they thought they knew was probably far less complicated than the facts and it was best to leave the explanations until he and Eloise knew what to explain.

'You could give Sam the tour,' Paul suggested, smiling at Eloise.

'The tour?' Sam had already been shown around the house.

'Yes, Gramps and I worked out a tour, as a fun thing to do for the house party. It takes in all of the hidden things that no one ever sees about the house.'

'Sounds interesting.'

'It is, very…' Aunt Celeste seemed to approve of the idea. 'The house has been around for so long that it's gathered up a lot of fascinating little foibles. There's a priest's hole…'

'I didn't know there was a priest's hole.

Where?' The tour was beginning to sound more interesting by the minute, particularly since his tour guide was so remarkably beautiful when she was brimming with excitement.

'Ah!' Eloise tapped the side of her nose. 'Come with me and I'll show you.'

It was the perfect excuse. Paul and Aunt Celeste had decided to go and check out the new Indian restaurant in town after an early showing of the film they wanted to see, and said that they wouldn't be home until nine o'clock. That gave Sam five hours alone with Eloise, in a house that had more spare bedrooms to explore than they could ever possibly need.

The house was chilly, which seemed to be its normal state during cold weather, but Eloise led him to the kitchen, which was always an island of warmth. She heated up some soup, from a seemingly inexhaustible supply in the freezer, and showed him the back of the pantry door.

'How old is some of this graffiti?' He ran his finger across the clear acrylic sheet that protected the door.

'We don't know about most of it. Some of it's pretty ageless.' Eloise pointed out a heart, scratched deeply into the wood, with two initials. 'Whoever *"EW"* and *"JP"* were, I hope they had a nice life together.'

So did Sam. Both he and Eloise knew that things didn't always work out the way you'd planned, but it suddenly seemed important that they had for these two anonymous lovers.

'But look—this one.' She pointed to a fainter inscription and Sam narrowed his eyes, trying to make it out.

'*"I left my leg..."* What's that...?'

'*"At Waterloo."* And his heart is here.'

'Ah, yes.' Sam could see now that this was what the wobbly script was saying. 'So that must be almost two hundred years old.'

Eloise nodded. 'This one's a bit more recent. It was written by Gramps' mother, at the end of the war. My great-grandmother.'

'*"VE Day, 8th May 1945. May God bless the peace."*' Sam grinned. 'It's all here, isn't it? Love, injury and loss...hope for the future.'

'Yes, that's what makes it so fascinating. We're not so very different from the people who wrote these. I'm here too. I remember Gramps taking the cover off and telling us that it was important we were there.'

A little lower down on the door, Paul's initials were there, along with those of his first wife. Underneath, three more groups of linked initials.

'That's my parents, John and Elizabeth Grant. Gramps helped me do my initials underneath, when I was eight years old. And look, there's Gramps again, with Celeste.'

Sam nodded. 'I remember Aunt Celeste telling me about that, when Paul first asked her to marry him. She said that she was very touched that he wanted to include her on the list of family names, but I didn't realise that it was on the back of a door.'

Eloise laughed. 'That's the thing about this house. It can be very grand, but it's the little things that mean the most. Come and see the priest's hole.'

She led him into the sitting room, and challenged him to find it. After taking the most obvious route, and rapping his knuckles on the wood panelling, Sam looked for secret levers in the fireplace and peered behind the bookcases.

'Okay, I give up.'

'You're sure? You haven't been near it yet...'

Sam looked around the room. The steps that led up to the first-floor gallery were a possibility, but the space beneath them was concealed by wood panelling and Sam couldn't find any openings that a man might slip through.

'You're getting warmer...' Eloise teased him, and Sam walked up the steps, knocking the stair risers as he went.

'I can't work it out.'

Eloise chuckled. 'You had the right idea. Here, let me show you.'

She joined him on the stairs, and ran her fingers along the edge of one of the wooden stair treads. A click sounded, as if a lever had been released, and Eloise swung the two top steps upwards to reveal a small cavity. Sam looked inside.

'That's no more than a couple of square feet. No-one could fit in there.'

Eloise laughed. 'Which is exactly what you're supposed to think. It's a hiding place for valuables, but at the back...

She pushed at the wooden beams at the back of the compartment and they swung to one side. Reaching in she flipped a switch and a light came on revealing a brick lined hidey-hole, extending downwards under the stairs.

'If anyone did work out how to lift the stairs they'd find the smaller cavity and most likely stop there. Even if they did investigate further, the beams can be secured from the inside so they won't move.'

Sam bent down to look. 'Clever. And if you

removed the wood panelling under the stairs, you'd just see a brick wall behind it.'

'Yes, that's right.'

'And this is the only one?'

'We've looked and we can't find any others—but then they're very cleverly concealed. Celeste had an idea of doing some kind of sonar survey, and Gramps is looking into how that might work, so maybe they'll find a few more.'

Sam took another look inside, wondering what it would be like to have to hide away in here. As he reached in to switch off the light he felt his hand snag painfully on something.

'Ow.' When he looked he saw blood. 'I think I found a nail.'

Eloise took his hand, inspecting the wound. 'Probably rusty if I know this place. Are you up to date on your tetanus jabs? I should have warned you that you need to be if you go exploring here.'

'I'll be fine. Although if you've got a plaster… Before I pass out from loss of blood.' Eloise had been squeezing the small cut and it had started to bleed more freely.

'Just making sure there's nothing in it.' She let go of his hand, and Sam followed her to the kitchen.

'Hold it under the tap.'

'That's what I'm about to do.' Two doctors fighting over one small cut had the potential to get ugly. Sam rinsed his finger, watching as Eloise reached up to one of the high cupboards, punching the combination lock before flipping open the door.

The cupboard was large and very full. Eloise was stretching to get a good view of the upper shelf and Sam turned the tap off, walking over to see if he could make out its contents any better.

'That's one of the things I like about Paul. He doesn't stint on medical supplies.'

'No, but I wish he'd organise them a bit better. *He* knows where everything is, but no one else can find anything.'

Sam reached up, moving some of the contents of the shelf to one side to get a better view. As he did so, two boxes became dislodged and fell out of the cupboard, and Eloise caught them.

'Ah, here we are. This one's plasters…' She fell silent and Sam was suddenly aware that he'd been standing very close to her. The other box contained condoms.

She dropped it suddenly, as if it would burn her, turning round quickly to face him. 'We don't need to worry about those, do we.' She opened the box of plasters, taking out the largest one.

No, they didn't. Sam held out his hand, and she somehow managed to apply the plaster without touching his skin. But her scent still caressed his senses, calling to him that any decision could be made at any time.

'Thanks. That's great.' It was one thing to know that the roads were clear now, and that Sam could get into his car and drive to find a chemist's shop that was open. It was quite another to have a box of condoms fall out of the cupboard. Sam had never felt that the fates had any sway over his life, but even he had to admit it was an awkward coincidence.

This was crazy. He didn't need to hide behind practicalities to control his own actions and desires.

Eloise picked up the box, turning it in her hand. When she came to the side that displayed a use-by date she was still again, and Sam couldn't help but notice that it was over a year away.

'I don't know what these are doing here anyway.' She stuffed the box back into the cupboard, slamming it shut, and Sam heard the lock engage. As if that made any difference. Eloise could open the cupboard back up any time she wanted…

He tried to tear his mind away from all of the possibilities that seemed to be leaving no room for anything else. 'So what's next on the tour?'

She was silent for a moment. 'The desk that Gramps put in Celeste's study has three secret compartments.'

'Three?'

'Yes. And the wall at the back of the property is part Roman. Gramps has extended it but he used contrasting stonework that complemented the Roman part, but also made it obvious that it was different.'

'Fascinating.' Eloise was fascinating. Her hair, her eyes. Her skin, and the way that her cheeks were flushed in the warmth of the kitchen. He could take or leave both the Roman wall and Paul's extension of it.

'It's cold outside, though. And if you wanted to stay here...?' Eloise took a step towards him. 'This place feels like home to me, Sam, and decisions I make here can't be left behind or thrown away. If you feel differently, then I won't mention it again.'

Right now, Eloise was the only truth that he could rely on. The only thing that seemed constant in a world that had thrown this challenge at him when he'd least expected it. Eloise wanted him and the sheer joy of that dissolved all of his fears. Sam didn't know how he would come to terms with wanting her as much as he did, but that seemed like an obstacle that could be surmounted now.

'Paul and Celeste won't be back for another four hours.' He knew that, almost to the minute, because he'd been counting the moments he had to spend alone in her company and valuing each one. 'There's nothing I'd like more than to spend that time in getting to know you better.'

Still, he couldn't make the first move. Consent wasn't a concept that Sam had ever struggled with. It was perfectly simple. There were no smudged lines, no difficulties in knowing whether a woman had made the decision that she wanted him. But his father's continual disregard of his mother's wishes had made Sam even more careful, wanting even more for it to be spoken in a way that gave no room for doubt.

Eloise was motionless for a moment. Maybe she'd give up on him and turn away, and he'd have to deal with that.

'Sam, I want you to take me upstairs and make love to me. Is that clear enough for you?'

She'd put two and two together and she understood. And he knew now too. In one swift movement he lifted her off her feet, perching her on the kitchen worktop. 'Give me the combination…'

Eloise was smiling now. 'Make me.'

He kissed her, feeling her body mould against his. Exquisite. Sam wondered how long it would take before she gave him the number, and hoped that she might hold out a little longer. He slid one hand around her back, covering her breast with the other. Even though she was wearing a thick sweater, and no doubt a couple more layers of clothes underneath, he heard her cry out.

'More, Sam.'

'You want to play this game?' He could do that. Pulling her hard against his body, so that she could feel just how much he wanted her, he slipped his hand under her sweater.

'Oh! You'll have to do better than that, though…'

He whispered exactly how much more he could do, and she wriggled against him. The feeling stoked the fire in his veins, and he described another scenario in slightly more detail.

'Sam! Three-seven-four-eight.'

'You're sure, now?' He held her close, planting kisses on her neck, finally managing to free his hand from the layers of clothes under her sweater, so that he could touch her skin. He let his fingers trail to the clasp on her bra, and then forward, to skim the softest skin of all.

'Three-seven-four-eight, Sam!' Her arms were clasped around his neck, and suddenly she let him go, pushing him away from her a little. He felt her hands move to the front of his jeans and almost choked with the intensity of his reaction to her touch.

'Do it!' She knew that she had the better of him, and her voice took on a commanding tone. Sam reached above her head, punching the combination into the lock and hooking the box of condoms out of the cupboard. Eloise took them from him, pushing him away as she slid forwards, planting her feet back on the floor.

'Come upstairs. Right now.'

CHAPTER TEN

SAM WASN'T INDECISIVE. It just seemed that her decisions, the things that she wanted, were more important to him. Eloise could see why. He'd grown up in a house where his father had consistently ignored his mother's wishes. This waiting, the hesitation were just proof that Sam was an honest man who she could respect, and she wanted him all the more for it.

She led him along the gallery to her own bedroom, wondering what he'd make of the high four-poster bed and hoping that it might give his imagination something to work with. As she opened the door, she felt chilly air on her face.

'Uh. The radiator's not working again. I thought that Gramps had fixed it. Perhaps we should go to yours…'

He sat down on the bed. 'It's okay. I'll keep you warm.'

This was a big step for both of them. They

were pulled together by powerful chemistry, despite all their caution over having been hurt. But, right now, it seemed that all they really needed to know was that they'd keep each other safe and warm. She walked over to him and he wrapped his arms around her.

That slow pace of his. The way he stretched out every moment into something delightful. Eloise had been with men who liked to start slow before, but Sam was so exquisitely good at it.

'I love to play a little first…' she whispered in his ear. 'Just so you know.'

He chuckled. 'I love the way you tell me exactly what you want. And I like to play too.'

It was a smooth, slow ascent to fever pitch. When Sam undressed her, he didn't rush, letting her feel the chill air on her skin, along with the heat of his body. If sex was all about different kinds of sensation, and Eloise reckoned that it was, then Sam was the man who could make the most of every one of the thrills running through her body.

Under the thick, heavy bedcovers he did things to her that made her blood begin to boil. Finally she called time on it.

'Sam… Sam, are you ready?'

She felt his breath, warm against her skin as he sighed. If he had any clue about how she was feeling, and she hadn't held back in telling him, it would be satisfaction at a job well done.

'I'm ready. You?' He rolled her over onto her back.

'More than you can ever imagine...'

He reached for the condoms. After the sharp longing and lazy pleasures of the last couple of hours, the delicious languor was broken. She felt his weight on her, and a sudden, warm feeling blooming through her as her body reacted to his and took him inside.

Sam was no longer hesitant, no longer needing any of her words to guide him. He'd found out exactly what she liked, and he seemed intent on hearing only incoherent sounds of pleasure. No one could resist this for very long, and she felt tears prick at the sides of her eyes as the long-awaited release began to build.

And then it happened. There were no words, because that would have been impossible. But Eloise could feel his every reaction, and Sam had suddenly broken free of that thoughtful, exquisite rhythm of his and surrendered to the moment. She heard him catch his breath, and knew that they were finally alone together, cut free from the past.

Just a little longer...

But it was too much to be able to control or to keep. Eloise felt Sam's body begin to stiffen and he held her tight as her orgasm drove everything else away, dragging him over the edge with her.

The intensity of it almost dazed her. Sharp aftershocks ran through her body, and Sam shifted, curling his arms around her. Words really didn't cover this. Nothing did. There had been no thought, just sheer emotion.

Had he felt it too? Eloise had no doubt that he had. Would he admit to it, though?

'Are you okay?'

That was a start. Whether he knew it or not, he'd just acknowledged that they'd gone beyond the bounds of what either of them had expected.

'Much better than okay. What did you do to me, Sam?'

'I was just wondering what you'd done to me...'

'I didn't...'

The truth started to seep in. Sam was a wonderful lover, he watched and listened, and did everything to please her. But they'd both glimpsed something more than that, something un-thought and instinctive. She hadn't done anything to make it happen, and neither had he.

'This is what happens between us, then. You and me together?' She wanted more. Now that she'd seen the place where nothing existed but Sam, she wanted it back.

'I suppose…' Sam's brow creased in thought. 'Maybe not every time.'

He didn't sound very convinced of that, and neither was Eloise. But this was their first time together, and they were only just getting to know each other. If she wanted to concentrate on something, then she should concentrate on the knowledge that Sam was the best lover she'd ever had. They probably weren't ready yet, for the brief moments of complete freedom they'd experienced. That would come in time.

'I really want to find out.'

Sam kissed her. 'Yes. Me too.'

He hadn't noticed that Eloise had set an alarm, but Sam was glad she had. They were dozing comfortably in her bed, warm as toast under the thick, heavy quilt, and Sam had forgotten all about Paul and Aunt Celeste coming home at nine. So, apparently, had Eloise, because she jumped to attention, sitting upright in the bed.

'Uh.' She rubbed her eyes. 'It's okay, we have half an hour…'

'Unless they're early,' Sam teased.

'They won't be. The film ends when it ends, and Gramps doesn't believe in rushing good food.' She frowned. 'Although the restaurant could turn out to be terrible, which might speed up their timetable.'

'Relax. What's the worst that could happen? They come home right now and find us in bed together. You refuse to apologise, and your grandfather locks you in your room and then takes me down to his study and shoots me.'

Eloise chuckled. 'He wouldn't do that. He really likes you.'

'He's really going to like the things you just did to me?' Sam raised an eyebrow and received a play punch in response.

'You did some things to me as well. I'm going to go and take a shower and wash off the evidence.' She got out of bed, and Sam watched as she skittered across the room, towards the oak door that led to the en-suite bathroom.

She was gorgeous. Mesmerising. They had a meeting of minds that had made the meeting of their bodies beyond anything that Sam could have imagined. If he *had* been able to imagine this, then he would have baulked at the loss of control. The raw intimacy that had lasted for only a moment, but had been far stronger than his resolve to always think about his actions and how they might affect his partner.

But there was no going back on something that had rocked his world so thoroughly. He had to own it, and have the courage to find out where it was going to go. Because the one thing that he'd been trying to avoid had happened, and Sam was committed.

They'd tidied up downstairs, closing the priest's hole and washing up the pan and mugs of half-drunk soup. The box of condoms was safely back in the medicine cabinet, and Aunt Celeste and Paul were fifteen minutes late.

And they'd come to a decision. An impromptu afternoon spent together was one thing, but creeping to Eloise's room tonight, when they were both guests in the house, was quite another. This might be a leap of faith that Sam wasn't entirely ready to make, but he had to think of Eloise now too. She wanted to tell Paul, needed to be honest with him, and so that was what Sam wanted as well.

'Hello you two.' Aunt Celeste stopped short at the kitchen door, sensing that something was up. 'What are you doing, sitting in here?'

'Nothing!' Eloise blurted out the word. That was essentially true. Sam had taken his hand from her shoulder, and was no longer leaning towards her to catch her gaze.

'Oh. Well, fair enough. The film was wonderful, wasn't it, Paul?'

'Yes, you must try and catch it down in London. I think we'll be going back to the restaurant again as well, eh, Celeste.'

'Definitely. The food was very tasty.' Celeste hung her coat on the back of one of the kitchen chairs. 'I could do with some hot chocolate now.'

'I'll make it.' Eloise seemed to have lost her nerve completely and went to stand, but Sam reached out, brushing her arm. She gave him a little nod, and sat back down again.

Aunt Celeste gave them a querying look and headed for the range, grabbing one of the saucepans from the shelf on her way. Paul sat down at the table opposite them, folding his hands together, and Eloise looked up at him.

'What's up, Eloise?'

'There is something I want to tell you…'

Paul had clearly worked that out. He nodded, and Sam decided that since Eloise had already committed to this conversation, he should step in and help.

'Eloise and I have decided we'd like to see

a little more of each other, when we go back to London.' Everyone ignored the clatter of the saucepan as Aunt Celeste dropped it onto the flagstones.

'See a little more of each other? You mean professionally?' Paul asked, his gaze on Eloise, obviously trying to gauge her reaction. Sam reached out, resting his hand on the back of Eloise's chair in an attempt to suggest an alternative, and Eloise straightened suddenly.

'No, darling! Professionally, my foot! They're going to be seeing a little more of each other *personally*,' Aunt Celeste interjected. 'I dare say they've been spending the afternoon seeing each other personally.'

Sam closed his eyes. Aunt Celeste's no-nonsense approach to life was usually a joy. Sometimes it wasn't. He jumped when Eloise suddenly spoke up for herself.

'Yes. We have.'

'Ah!' Paul scratched his head, seeming perplexed. 'And you're happy about that?'

'Yes, Gramps.'

That was good to hear. If he'd thought for one moment that Eloise had any regrets about this afternoon he would have had to order himself out of the house in deep disgrace, before Paul got the chance to do it for him.

'Well, that's a piece of nice news, isn't it,

Paul?' Aunt Celeste picked up the saucepan, inspecting it for dents. 'There's something about the Douglases and the Grants, isn't there? When we're not at each other's throats, we get on very well indeed.'

Paul chuckled amiably. 'It seems so. Hurry up with the hot chocolate, darling, and we'll drink a toast to that.'

The radiator in Eloise's room seemed to be mysteriously working again, and was warming the place up now. Sam sat in the armchair by the window, looking at the bed, the covers pulled straight now to give no clue as to what had happened there.

Paul had beckoned Eloise into the sitting room, and she'd whispered to him to wait for her here before going to talk to her grandfather. Sam had little doubt that the conversation had something to do with his and Eloise's relationship and, even though Paul had seemed quite happy with the news, there was still that slight unease that came with knowing that people were talking about him.

He heard Aunt Celeste's footsteps on the stairs and then those of Eloise and Paul, still talking quietly. Then the door opened and she walked over to him.

'Hey you.' She smiled, sitting down on his knee.

'You're looking thoughtful. Are you okay?' Sam curled his arms around her shoulders and suddenly the world seemed right again.

'Yes, I am. Gramps wanted to ask me if I was happy.'

'I don't blame him. I was wondering the same thing.'

Eloise leaned up, kissing his cheek. 'You make me happy, Sam. If I seem to be fighting it a little, it's because I can't believe my luck in having met you.'

Yeah. He was fighting it too. But when they were together like this, it didn't seem so much of a battle.

'You told Paul that?'

'I told him that this last year hasn't been easy, but that I really want to leave it behind. And he's really pleased for us.'

The question that had been bothering Sam just had to be asked. It *could* be asked when he was holding her, because Eloise gave him the strength to try to believe in the future.

'What would you have done if he hadn't approved? If Aunt Celeste hadn't.'

She pursed her lips. 'I would have told you that you couldn't come to my room tonight. It's Gramps' house, after all, and we're guests.

I would have told *him* that I was leaving with you and that I'd stay with you, because that's my choice to make.'

'Good answer.' That was exactly what Sam had wanted to hear. That Eloise was able to break free from the past and give him some of the security that he craved, in a relationship that was already fraught with uncertainty.

'You were thinking I might give you up, just because someone told me to? Where's your faith in me, Sam?'

'I have faith. I can see how hard it might be to lose practically everyone over one relationship, and then see the one person who's stood by you disapprove of another.'

'Gramps trusts me and I should have trusted him a bit more in return.' Her eyes danced mischievously and she shifted in his arms, feeling under her sweater to pull something from the pocket of her skirt.

'He gave you those?' Sam chuckled when he saw the packet of condoms.

'Just in case we hadn't been able to get to the shops. I told him that if he looked inside he'd see that there were already some missing.'

Fair enough. At least Eloise had thought to mention that they were being sensible. Sam wondered whether it would be appropriate to have a man-to-man chat with Paul and tell him that he'd throw himself out of the nearest window rather than harm her.

'And what did he say?'

'He said he was glad that we were being responsible. Sometimes he thinks I'm still seventeen, it's really rather sweet of him.' She snuggled against Sam's chest. 'Are you going to be sweet to me now?'

'Would you like me to be?'

'Yes, I would. And I'd like to return the favour as well. Find out all of the things that you like.'

That was a little more challenging. Sam wasn't altogether comfortable about asking for what he wanted, because his father had done that so vociferously, and expected his mother to just give in to his every whim.

'I like your pleasure. Very much.' He kissed her and thoughts of his dysfunctional family dissolved suddenly. 'Let me make tonight all about you.'

Sam was amazing. Finding a man who could make a night all about her—who wouldn't want that? And he'd clearly enjoyed it, generous in his own lovemaking and finding his passion in the way that he carefully attended to hers.

There was more, and they both knew it

now. Eloise could wait, until Sam felt confident enough to tell her what *he* wanted.

Waking up wasn't an orderly process any more. Tasting the dregs of a dream, and realising that it *was* only a dream and the real world was still there. Dozing a little and then deciding it was time to get out of bed.

With Sam, it was more a matter of sitting bolt upright in bed and realising that they'd stayed too long in each other's embrace and should be somewhere else. Or just deciding that they could face the music later, because the only urgency seemed to be the one that she felt in his arms.

Eloise had checked out the upstairs hallway, and Sam had gone back to his room to shower and dress. He'd be leaving for London today, and she was already missing him. Already wondering what would happen when she followed him, tomorrow. When she went downstairs, she found a note on the kitchen table in Celeste's handwriting.

The hospital doesn't need us and it's a beautiful morning, so we've gone out for a walk. xx

Short and to the point. Eloise smiled. Celeste had probably decided that she and Sam might like to have breakfast alone—Gramps wouldn't have thought of that on his own—but she wasn't going to make a thing of it. She and Gramps were probably out somewhere making snowmen. Eloise called up to Sam, and he appeared at the top of the stairs.

'We've got the place to ourselves. Gramps and Celeste have gone out for a walk, so we can canoodle over breakfast.'

'That's nice of them.' He joined her at the bottom of the stairs. 'Have they called the hospital?'

'They must have done. Celeste says we're not needed there. We could have some toast and coffee and go out and find them if you like. They won't have gone far.'

'Nah.' He bent to kiss her. 'This winter we can concentrate on sitting around the fire and sweet nothings. Next year's soon enough for building snowmen.'

'You think so?' Firelight and sweet nothings *did* sound a lot more attractive at the moment. But the mention of even a tomorrow seemed huge at the moment. 'There's going to be a next year?'

He looked down at her thoughtfully. 'I honestly can't say, but I hope so. We'll have to wait and see.'

This was all so new. It all felt so delicious

and yet so very precarious. Trusting in anything felt as if it was a dangerous game, but the sweet chemistry between them, the way that Sam seemed to understand her made hope agonisingly easy.

She didn't get the chance to tell him how much she wanted next year because there was the sound of voices at the front door, and when Sam went to open it Gramps and Celeste were kicking snow from their boots in the porch.

'Ah, you're up.' Celeste's face was pink and cheery. 'Do you want to come and build a snowman? I can't believe we don't have one yet.'

'No…' Sam swung round, grinning at her as they both spoke together and then turned to Celeste.

'Thanks for the offer, but we'll stay in the warm. I think it's my turn to make breakfast, isn't it…?'

CHAPTER ELEVEN

SAM HAD PACKED his case and gone out to put it into the car. He'd kissed Celeste and shaken Gramps' hand, thanking them again and congratulating them on a weekend that hadn't quite turned out as planned, but was all the better for it. Then Gramps and Celeste disappeared into the kitchen, leaving Eloise to put on her coat and walk with him to his car, past the four new snowmen that stood at the front of the house. Gramps and Celeste had insisted they come outside and Sam had made an impressive snowman with broad shoulders and pieces of coal for its eyes. Eloise had made a smaller one, donating her second favourite hat for it to wear.

Sam leant back against the door of the car, putting his arm around her.

'I won't be kissing any snowmen while you're gone. Not even the handsome ones.' Eloise bit her tongue. She knew that Sam didn't like even the smallest insinuation that he might be jealous, but on this occasion he didn't seem to mind.

'Especially not handsome ones.' He even made a joke of it, pulling her close and resting his cheek against the top of her head. 'I'm working tomorrow. You're driving back to London in the afternoon?'

'Yes, that's the plan.'

'Well…if you feel like dropping round to my place in the evening… Or if it's too soon…'

Sam's diffidence again. He always gave her a choice, and sometimes that sounded as if he didn't really care. Eloise was learning that he was just doing what the past had taught him.

'I'd love to. Only… I don't know your address.'

He laughed suddenly. 'Come to think of it, I don't know yours either. I'll text you when I get home, and you can text me back with yours.'

'Do that.' A text from Sam, letting her know that he was home safe, was something else to look forward to. She stretched up, kissing him, and watched as he got into his car and drove away.

When she walked back to the house, Celeste was in the kitchen making tea. A banging from upstairs told Eloise that Gramps was probably using a mallet on one of the radiators to restore it to working order.

'We're going to have to do something about those old radiators. Paul insists he knows what he's doing, but I've told him that a heating system is nothing like the human body and we should call a plumber. Maybe summertime's best though.'

Eloise sat down at the table. 'Yes, you don't want people taking your heating system apart in this weather. I expect they're just full of air, or sludge or something, and Gramps is just moving it around with all that banging.'

'Yes, probably.' Celeste put a cup of tea down in front of her and sat down. 'There's something I want to say to you, Eloise.'

Sam. A shiver of unease crawled up Eloise's spine. She tried to hold onto the warmth, hold onto all the optimism, but it seemed that Sam had taken that with him, along with the rest of his luggage.

'What is it?' She hardly dared ask. It would be easy enough to duck the conversation. A muffled curse had sounded from upstairs and she could always pretend to go and see whether Gramps was all right. He obviously was, because the banging had started up again.

But if Sam had left nothing else, he'd left a measure of courage behind him, and she could at least do him the honour of listening to what Celeste had to say.

'It wasn't my place, but I told Sam about the business with Michael, when we were driving down here. I didn't mean to interfere, and personally I think you're better off without him and did the right thing…' Celeste puffed out a breath.

'Sam told me that you were planning a pincer movement, to save me from anyone who decided to give me a hard time.'

'Did he? Well, it's kind of him to assume that I had something that sophisticated up my sleeve. But Sam's a good man and he means a very great deal to me. I know he'd be furious if he thought that someone was being bullied and I'd kept quiet about it.'

'I appreciate it, Celeste, thank you. It was a kind gesture, and…some of the decisions I've made haven't been exactly good ones.'

'It's absolutely up to you who you marry, and what you choose to say about it. Paul tells me that he said much the same to you.'

'Yes, he did. Maybe I shouldn't have sworn Gramps to silence. I appreciate the way you've stood up for me…'

Celeste shot her a quizzical look. 'You

think Paul told me what to think? He did, of course, but I'd already come to my own conclusions. I don't know if you remember, but your wedding was the first time that I was his official plus one. I was keeping my mouth shut and my eyes skinned in case any of the Grants decided to come at me with a hatchet.'

Eloise laughed. Celeste just loved to play the old rivalry up a bit. 'I remember. We were all dying to catch a glimpse of you and I told one of the ushers to seat you and Gramps by the aisle, so I could see you from there.'

'Well, sometimes you can see things a little more clearly from the outside of a group of people, and it seemed to me that this Michael character was far too keen on telling a long story and getting everyone's sympathy. Most people aren't that charming when they're as heartbroken and innocent as he purported to be. When you came home, and you were clearly very upset about everything, and completely at a loss, I reckoned I knew who was in the right.'

Eloise reached for Celeste's hands. 'I don't know what Gramps has done to deserve you but, whatever it was, I'm really glad it worked. Thank you.'

Celeste chuckled. 'I'm glad that whatever I did to deserve Paul worked too. Even if he has lured me away to creaks in the night and heating that only works sometimes.'

'There's one place in the house that's always warm. It's my secret thinking place, and I don't think Gramps even knows I go there. Would you like to see it?'

The look in Celeste's eyes told Eloise that she knew exactly how this was meant. 'Thank you, darling. I'd love to.'

Eloise got to her feet, leading Celeste to the Great Hall.

One long night, and a very busy day, hadn't taken the edge off Sam's longing. He wanted to see Eloise more than he could say, and also rather more than he ought to. He trusted her, but it was still hard trying to be the man that she deserved. Someone who would love her and never hurt her.

He would find a way. Eloise had told him that she wanted their lovemaking to be about him as well as her, and in the brief moments that thought deserted him he'd found something precious. Something that had transcended anything he'd ever done before. He had to do what he thought was right, though.

But he could text her, and they'd spent an hour talking to each other last night. And

Eloise would be arriving back in London this evening and driving straight to his place.

His phone rang and one look at the display made him turn the corners of his mouth down. This was the one night that he didn't want the evening receptionist at the surgery to contact him.

'Hey there, Maria. What's up?'

'I'm *really* sorry, Sam. Mrs Cornelius has called, and she was crying… I expect it's just a repeat of the Christmas Tree Incident…'

Mrs Cornelius hadn't called since then, apart from ringing to thank Sam for sending such a nice woman round, and telling him that she was going to try out a community centre that she'd recommended. Sam wasn't so sure that this was nothing.

'That's okay. She wants to see me?'

'She asked for you. I can speak to Dr Chowdhary instead.'

'He's got more than enough on his plate already with the evening surgery.' The snow was never as deep in London as in other parts of the country, but the heat of the city meant that snow melted and then froze as ice. There were still plenty of patients with weather-related injuries to deal with. 'I'll go.'

Sam made for the front door, grabbing his coat and putting everything that was set out on the kitchen counter back in the fridge on the way. He texted Eloise to tell her that he'd been called away to a patient and would be back as soon as he could. She would understand.

She *would* understand, wouldn't she? He twisted the spare door key from his keyring, ready to slip it into its hiding place for Eloise to let herself in. And then he heard the lift doors open and saw Eloise, staring at her phone.

'No...! Tonight of all nights...' She turned the corners of her mouth down in disappointment.

'I'm so sorry.' Sam was upset too, and trying not to show it.

'Can't be helped.' She smiled suddenly, the cocktail of every kind of emotion leaving Sam unsure of how to respond. 'Where are you going? I can come with you if you like.'

'Mrs Cornelius—the Christmas Tree lady. But don't you want to wait in the flat? You can check things out while I'm gone.'

Eloise rolled her eyes. 'The only thing I want to check out is *you,* Sam.'

The lift doors began to close and she waved her hand impatiently across the sensor to open them again. Then she reached forward, grabbing the front of his jacket and pulling him into the lift.

'Come along. Don't keep her waiting…'

No, he shouldn't keep Mrs Cornelius waiting, but the time it took the lift to creak down the five floors to the basement car park was all his. When she pulled him close, his conflicting emotions lent a demanding edge to his kiss and he drew back.

'Don't keep *me* waiting, Sam.' She murmured the words. He kissed her again, feeling the thrill of his own demands couple with the urgency of hers.

The lift jolted to a halt too soon. Taking hold of her hand, he hurried to his car, wondering what had just happened. Why Eloise was the only woman he'd ever met who spurred such desire in him, and how she seemed to take pleasure in that.

'I'm… I'm disappointed too. A little cross, even…' He ventured the suggestion as he flipped the remote to unlock the car.

'I know.' She gave him a luminous smile that made Sam's heart lurch in his chest and got into the passenger seat.

There were three sets of traffic lights between his flat and Mrs Cornelius's. Sam knew that because the lights had been against them on two occasions and, instead of drumming his fingers on the steering wheel, he'd turned for a glimpse of that smiling connection between them before he put the car back into gear, ready to drive.

Mrs Cornelius lived on the top floor of a small block of flats and was a long time answering the door. Eloise turned, resting her ear against it.

'I can't hear anyone moving around.' She pressed the bell again.

'Maybe a neighbour has the key. Or, if the worst comes to the worst, I have a crowbar in the boot of the car...'

'Wait.' Eloise bobbed down, looking through the letterbox. 'I can see her feet. She's on her way...'

Slowly. It was another minute before Mrs Cornelius opened the door, which was longer than it took Sam to make a diagnosis. When he glanced at Eloise, she nodded her agreement.

'Hello, Mrs Cornelius. It's Sam, remember me?' He stepped inside, taking Mrs Cornelius's arm, in case she was unsteady on her feet. 'And this is Eloise, she's a doctor too.'

'Two of you. Am I that ill?' Mrs Cornelius's speech was slurred, but she could still speak. That was good, because all of the other signs, her drooping lip and one hand hanging uselessly at her side, indicated that she'd had a stroke.

Eloise gave her a scintillating smile. 'No, you're not that ill. Just that important.'

She stood back, watching, as Sam helped Mrs Cornelius into the sitting room. Everything she did, the way she moved. Eloise was storing everything away in her head, getting a complete picture of which parts of Mrs Cornelius's brain had been affected.

And Mrs Cornelius was watching too, her bright blue eyes fixed on Eloise's red coat and hat as Sam sat her carefully down on the sofa.

'I'll call an ambulance. You see if you can find out a bit more...'

Eloise nodded. Bending down in front of Mrs Cornelius, she took her hand. 'This is a bit scary, isn't it. But we're going to make sure that you're okay. Is it all right if I take you through a couple of things, to check out how you're feeling?'

Mrs Cornelius nodded. 'I like your hat...'

'Thank you.' Eloise chuckled, taking off the hat and putting it in Mrs Cornelius's lap. 'I sewed a white fur bobble onto it, because I made it for Christmas. It's really soft...'

Mrs Cornelius's hand moved to the hat, probably just as Eloise had intended. Sam turned away, dialling the number for the emergency services. By the time he'd got through, Eloise already had some of the information he needed.

'She says she's been feeling like this for about an hour and a half. She made dinner for herself and sat down and ate it. Then her next-door neighbour popped in…what time was that, Joy? About five o'clock?' She glanced at Mrs Cornelius, who nodded.

'Okay, I'll go and check.' It was important to know what time the stroke had started to take hold, because clot busters might be a treatment option when Mrs Cornelius got to the hospital. Sam relayed the information to the emergency operator, and went to knock next door to see if he could find the neighbour who had seen her.

He struck lucky on the first door. The young woman who answered had been in to see whether Mrs Cornelius wanted a lift to the shops at the weekend, and she confirmed that she'd seemed fine and was showing none of the symptoms that Sam asked about.

'She'll have to go to the hospital?'

'Yes, we've called an ambulance and it's on its way.'

'I'll go with her.' The woman called over her shoulder, 'Odette, it's Mrs Cornelius.

From what the doctor says she's had a stroke and needs to go to the hospital. I'm going to go with her...'

Sam hadn't actually said anything about a stroke, but most people knew the symptoms and he guessed that his line of questioning made it pretty obvious. He went back to Mrs Cornelius's flat, telling the neighbour to knock when she was ready.

Eloise got to her feet, her gaze still on Mrs Cornelius as she spoke to Sam. 'She has obvious facial weakness, and she can't raise her right arm at all. Her speech is a little slurred but she's able to form the words, and I gave her a pen and paper and she wrote her name and address down.'

'Good. I've spoken to the neighbour and she says that she was fine at five, no symptoms then. She says she'll go to the hospital with her. The ambulance is on its way, they reckon fifteen minutes.'

'Great. What's the neighbour's name?'

'No idea.'

Eloise gave him a grin. 'Okay, I'll manage.'

She squatted back down in front of Mrs Cornelius, who was stroking the bobble on her hat, the other hand lying useless in her lap.

'Joy, Sam's been next door to talk to your neighbour. He didn't get her name...'

'Odette and Frankie.' Mrs Cornelius supplied the information, which no doubt went into Eloise's mental notes straight away.

'Frankie, then. She called to Odette,' Sam added.

'All right, so we're pretty sure you're going to need to go to the hospital, to get some treatment. Frankie says she'd like to go with you—would you like that?'

'Yes… Yes, I'd like Frankie to come with me. Does Sam know what's wrong with me?'

Since Eloise had done most of the diagnostic work, Sam reckoned that she would be allowed to feel a little indignant. But her smile never wavered.

'Yes, he does. And you know that Sam's a great doctor, right? He doesn't miss anything, so you called the right person to come and see you.'

Mrs Cornelius nodded, tears welling in her eyes and falling down her cheeks. She tried to wipe them away with her hand, and Eloise produced a clean tissue from her handbag.

'All right, my love. It's all right.' She gently wiped Mrs Cornelius's face and then hugged her, in a gesture that was completely non-standard in any rule book he'd ever seen, but nonetheless immensely effective.

By the time the ambulance arrived, Sam

had called the surgery and had a set of notes and Mrs Cornelius's medical history to pass on to the paramedic. Frankie was sitting next to her on the sofa, holding her hand. He saw Eloise put her hat onto Mrs Cornelius's head as the ambulance crew got ready to go, telling her that she couldn't go out without something to keep her head warm.

They watched as the ambulance drew away and then Eloise took his arm. 'I think she's going to be okay, Sam. She has a good chance. I've seen people come into A&E who are a lot worse than this, and who recover well.'

He narrowed his eyes. 'And how would you know that? I thought that A&E was a matter of doing your best for people and moving on.'

She shot him an innocent look. 'Following up, to gauge the effectiveness of our treatment, is an integral part of the process, I'll have you know.'

'Of course.' Sam smiled down at her. 'Along with the giving of hats.'

Eloise aimed a play punch at his arm. 'I like to maintain patients' spirits when they're in an emergency situation, whenever I can. And I've got loads of hats. I can always knit another one.'

'You knit?' Sam knew exactly how to give

Eloise pleasure, but he had to admit that he knew very little else about her.

'Yes, it's a great way to relax in the evening. Sitting down with my needles in front of the fire.'

'Don't let me stop you, then. If you want to go home and get started on a replacement...'

'And let you eat alone?' She plucked a supermarket sticker from the sleeve of his coat, that must have transferred when he was putting everything back into the fridge and gone unnoticed. 'Free range steak. Very nice.'

'It's about the only thing I can cook.' He grinned down at her.

'Since Celeste tells me you can't cook *anything* that doesn't either go in the oven or the microwave, then that's a lot better than I was expecting.'

'Oh, so you've been interrogating Aunt Celeste, have you?'

'Yep. Twenty-seventh of July.'

'Correct. Anything else?'

'No, that's it. I know your birthday and that you can't cook. I actually don't even know how old you are.'

'Thirty-five. You?'

'Thirty-two. See, this getting-to-know-you process is really quite painless.'

Sam hoped so. They'd shared so much, but

so little, before tumbling headlong into an affair. They couldn't go back now. They just had to trust in the connection that had sparked between them, right from the start.

'So…' He unlocked the car, opening the passenger door for her. 'I'm offering you the chance to come home with me and find out a bit more about me. And warm your ears, of course.'

'I accept. Particularly the ear warming part…'

CHAPTER TWELVE

SAM'S TRANSFORMATION OF the Great Hall hadn't been a chance stroke of luck. He had an eye for interiors, and his flat was gorgeous. Part of a block built in the nineteen-twenties, he'd echoed the theme of the curved windows and Art Deco fireplaces with light fittings and other accessories of the same style. But he hadn't stuck slavishly to the theme, he'd just added furniture that complemented the space, and in breaking all of the rules he'd made something that was both stylish and all his own. His solid oak bedroom suite would have been at home in any modern setting, but the clean lines complemented the ornate fireguard that stood in front of a cast iron fireplace.

'This is beautiful, Sam.' She sat down on the bed, finding that it was very comfortable too. 'My decorating style is more whatever fits in the car.'

He chuckled. 'That works. Feel free to try out the bed any time you like.'

'I was wondering if you'd like me to try out your cooker first.'

'Do you mind?'

'No, I love cooking and I don't do enough of it, living on my own. You can watch and learn. I also like eating, so I reckon this is an investment in my future.' Eloise took his hand, pulling him to sit down next to her on the bed.

He held her hand between his, staring down at it. 'Is this going too fast, Eloise?'

It *did* all seem to have happened at the speed of light. They'd been stuck in the snow, with nothing of their real lives to hold on to, but still they'd connected, both physically and emotionally. They'd laughed at each other's jokes, and seen things through each other's eyes. Sam understood her, and she felt that she understood him.

'Maybe. But I'm going to stick with it, because I've never had anything like this happen to me before. I can't let go of you now, Sam, just because it's happened so quickly.'

He smiled suddenly. 'I can't let go of you either.'

'And tomorrow evening you can come to my place, and move the furniture around a bit if you like, I'll learn something from you. It would be really boring if we found that we were just the same, wouldn't it?'

He lifted her hand to his lips, kissing it. 'I won't move a thing, Eloise. It'll be perfect, just as you are.'

The last three weeks had been amazing. During the week, there wasn't much time for anything other than a couple of hours' relaxation and then tumbling into bed together, but they'd made the most of it. They'd talked, picked books to read from each other's shelves, listened to each other's music. She'd seen photographs of when Sam was little, although the expected ones of a young child with his father seemed to be missing, and Eloise had shown him hers.

The weekends were different. Two days to explore all of the things they loved about London. Sam took her to the National Gallery, and his knowledge about art and paintings made everything seem to come alive in a way that paint on canvas never had before. Eloise took him to her favourite markets, knitting him a hat to keep him warm as they browsed the stalls. They went to the cinema and tried different restaurants. Eloise gritted her teeth and climbed to the top of Tower Bridge with him, but couldn't hide her dizziness when she looked down through the glass-floored walkways. Sam had to admit that he never ate fish, after going to a sushi bar to meet with a group of Eloise's friends. It was as if life was once more beginning to circle them with the protective shield of everyday checks and balances.

He'd given her so much, and now she was going to ask for the one thing that he'd held back from giving her. It was Friday evening, and they had the weekend ahead of them. Now was the time to take another step in their relationship.

'Sam, I want to talk to you. About sex.'

'That's a great subject to start the weekend off with. Shall we take this into the bedroom?' He took a couple of glasses from the kitchen cupboard and reached for the bottle of wine he'd just taken out of the refrigerator.

'No. Let's talk here.' Eloise sat down at the kitchen table. She'd thought carefully about this, and decided that a serious conversation about sex was best had out of the bedroom. And probably not in the sitting room either, where comfortable chairs and the sofa had already provided them with temptation that hadn't been resisted.

'Okay.' Sam frowned, putting the bottle and

glasses aside and sitting down. 'Do we have a problem?'

'No, I love every moment of the time we spend together. In and out of bed.'

'I love it too. There's no reason why we can't love it a little more.' He seemed tense now, choosing his words carefully. Eloise had hoped that the conversation might be a little easier than this was shaping up to be.

'Yes, and it's nothing bad, Sam.' She reached for his hand and held it tight. 'You're the lover I've always wanted, someone who cares about what I'm feeling and what I want…'

'I'm sensing there's a *but* coming.' That tenderness that she loved so much showed in his face. 'Just tell me. We can put this right.'

Sam meant that *he* would put it right. He'd do whatever it took to make her happy, he'd already made that clear in his words and his actions. Eloise took a breath. Sometimes there was nothing for it but to come out and say exactly what you meant.

'I want to make *you* happy, Sam. You hear my fantasies then you make them real, and it's amazing. I want to do the same for you.'

A pulse beat at the side of his brow now. Eloise had known that getting through to him about this wouldn't be easy, but she hadn't realised it would be so hard. How much Sam had invested in the belief that he had to work every day to be nothing like his father.

'Let me be the one who hears you sometimes, Sam. That's what I really want.'

She just had to trust that he would understand, because Michael hadn't when she'd challenged his view of how their relationship ought to be. That there should be no secrets and that there was room for his son in their lives. Sam was the better man, and Eloise had to trust in that.

She could almost hear him thinking. In the silence, the quiet tick of the clock and the distant noise of traffic suddenly became very loud.

'You're not talking about just the bedroom, are you?'

He was very astute. Conversations with Sam had a tendency to turn into more than she'd bargained for.

'What happens there is a reflection of everything else. The balance of our relationship...'

Sam nodded. 'I'm not sure that I know how to change that.'

'It's up to us both, not just you. I know you listen to what I want and how I feel, and

I have to trust that. Trust myself to be able to say what's really on my mind.'

Eloise had done that once and her heart had been broken. That was over now. Michael was gone and she was glad that she hadn't made the mistake of marrying him. But since then she'd learned the habit of keeping her thoughts to herself.

He reached out suddenly, holding his hands open on the table. 'Hold on to me. I promise I'll hold on to you.'

That was what she really needed right now. She took his hands, and his fingers curled around hers. Warm and secure, the way he always made her feel.

'Telling me what you want doesn't make you like your father, Sam.'

She felt his grip tighten. Holding on to her still. Sam shrugged, puffing out a breath.

'All we ever used to hear when we were kids was what my father wanted, and he put Mum through a very hard time when the marriage broke up. Afterwards she told me that one of her reasons for staying strong was that she wanted to show us kids that the way he acted wasn't how a man should act.'

'She sounds like a strong woman, who defended her children. Hard act to follow.'

Surprise showed in his eyes. Then he nodded. 'Yeah, maybe… You think I try too hard?'

'I think you don't need to try, Sam. You've seen all of the things that happen when a man tries to take control of his family, and all of the heartbreak that causes. You've rejected that and you're not like your father.'

'I may need a moment to think about that…'

'That's okay. This isn't an ultimatum. I want you to think about it.' That was another challenge for both of them to consider. They couldn't just turn their backs on this, however much she was afraid of losing what they had. Sam had to know that she wasn't just going to disappear and leave him not knowing what had happened between them.

'Eloise…' There was such warmth in his eyes. Such feeling. 'I think I'm falling in love with you. Actually… I'm pretty certain that I am.'

'I'm pretty certain I'm falling in love with you too, Sam. So let's make sure we get this right.'

There was no lack of warmth about the evening. Touching, kissing. Laughing together. The intimacy between them was about as close as Eloise had ever been to sex with her clothes on, and it was very close. Giving him time to think, removing the expectation that they'd be going to the bedroom at any moment, had somehow made *not* going to the bedroom very special.

Sam went as far as asking her whether she minded if he just held her tonight. It was what he wanted, what felt right to him at the moment, and Eloise wanted that more than anything. She propped herself up on the pillows in the bedroom wearing a T-shirt and pair of shorts that she kept here for lazy Sunday mornings, fiddling with the remote on the TV as a way of not noticing that he too was getting changed.

'Do you fancy a film?' She handed the remote to him.

'Yeah...' He flipped through the programme list. 'This?'

'No, not in the mood for gritty realism. I've been doing that all week.'

He chuckled. 'Good point. This...?' He found a feature length cartoon animation.

'Yes. Perfect.'

He paused for a moment, before he started the film.

'You know. There's always consent...'

Eloise chuckled. 'You mean that thing we've just been doing?'

Sam frowned. 'It's a bit more important

than just deciding what film we want to watch, isn't it?'

'Yes, of course it is. You know the difference between yes and no?'

'Yes, I do.'

'I know how to say either of them, Sam. At any time.'

He nodded, putting his arm around her shoulders and pressing the remote to start the film.

This was the most unexpected thing that anyone had ever done. Sam had grown up knowing what he didn't want to be, and not thinking too much about what he *did* want. He'd told himself that he would always respect a woman's wishes, and that he must listen well to achieve that. And then Eloise had turned all of that on its head. She'd told him he was good enough already, and that she wanted to listen and fulfil some of his wishes.

But that was why he loved her. He knew their conversation had been hard for her, but he'd seen a new determination in Eloise. She didn't want to settle for what was comfortable, or even something that was amazingly good. She wanted the things he hadn't known how to give, and made them feel possible.

She'd started to yawn, and Sam had turned

the TV off. Then he'd asked the question that he hadn't known he could risk asking, because it allowed for everything he'd been dreading. Stepping back for a moment and reconsidering gave her the opportunity to slip away from him.

'Will you give me some time…?'

'As much as you want, Sam. I'm not going anywhere.'

They slept, curled up in the bed together. Warm, comfortable and secure. And out of that security came the feeling that if he loved her well enough, then he could learn to combine his own desires with hers. It had happened once before, on their first night together, and he'd been trying not to think about it ever since.

Sam woke as the first feeble light of morning began to disturb the darkness. Quiet sounds of movement from the bathroom made him wonder momentarily what day it was, and then he remembered it was Saturday.

And Eloise was already up? Then he remembered last night. She was just giving him the space that he'd asked for. She knew as well as he did what usually happened when they woke up together on their days off.

By the time she tiptoed back into the bedroom, barefooted and wrapped in a towel, her hair wound loosely at the back of her head, he was fully awake. Eloise glanced in his direction, turning the corners of her mouth down.

'Did I wake you?'

'No, I've been waiting for you to come back.' Maybe Eloise would take the hint, drop the towel and get back into bed.

She gave him an amused look, obviously not in the mood for hints this morning. Walking over to the wardrobe, she flipped the door open to reveal the full-length mirror fixed inside, pulling her hair down.

It was difficult to know whether she meant this as a come-on, because everything she did fascinated Sam. But suddenly he knew exactly what he wanted. It wasn't so outrageous, and nothing they hadn't done before. The really shocking thing about it was the idea that he wasn't going to just wait and hope she might ask.

He got out of bed, standing behind her and winding his arms around her waist. As he dropped a kiss on her neck, he felt her fingers close around his wrists, holding them in place. She must be able to feel how aroused he was, because she moved against him, her gaze meeting his in the mirror.

'That's nice…' She seemed to melt into his

arms as he kissed her shoulder. Everything…
everything told him that this was exactly what
she wanted, but still he had to ask.

'You want to make love?'

'Yes. What do you want, Sam?'

The question emboldened him. Sam pulled
the towel away, letting it drop to the floor. His
hands skimmed her body and she leaned back
against him, closing her eyes.

'I'd like it if you watched…'

Her eyes snapped open, meeting his gaze in
the mirror. 'I'd like it if you lost the T-shirt…'

Sam pulled his T-shirt off. He wound his
arms around her, one hand on her breast and
the other travelling slowly downwards.

'Sam!' Her gaze was still fixed on his reflection in the mirror, and he felt her begin to
tremble. His desire, along with hers, tangling
together to make something that they'd only
glimpsed before now.

Slowly, gently, because he wanted to see
her face as passion took hold of her, he started
to move his fingers. Locked in this embrace,
in this moment, he suddenly understood just
what surrender was. There were no fears, no
doubts, just the certain knowledge that what
he wanted was as much of a turn-on for Eloise as it was for him.

'This may take a while.' He whispered the words and felt her shudder of delight.

'Yes. Sam, please… I really want you to take your time…'

It had been amazing. Eloise had never felt such longing for anyone, never felt such complete surrender. Sex with Sam had always been the best she'd ever had, but this was so far off the scale that there wasn't even a way of comparing.

He'd loved it too. Sam's newfound confidence had allowed her own to blossom. When he'd lain back, telling her that the next time she came he wanted her to take him with her, she'd felt a new kind of freedom, a new pleasure in her own assertiveness because it was now a part of his.

She snuggled against him, holding him tight. 'I think we're getting better as we go, Sam.'

Eloise felt him kiss the top of her head. 'Maybe we should just agree on stopping here, eh?'

Really? 'You don't want to do this again?'

'No, I mean stopping to explore this idea. Explore each other a little more and who we really are. Really getting to know all of the possibilities.' He was laughing at her consternation.

'Ah. Yes, I think we could find lots of possibilities. Not right now, you understand.'

Sam chuckled. 'No, I think I'm temporarily out of possibilities. We do have the whole weekend, though.'

'My thoughts exactly…'

Sam had never been happier. In the two weeks since that marvellous, explosive weekend, when they'd not moved from his flat, they'd been finding their place together. Somewhere that it was safe for him to express his own wants and needs, and where Eloise could trust that her own past was where it should be— not forgotten but in the past. And since the laws of physics didn't seem to apply to the way that he loved her, having more room for his own desires and feelings left more room for Eloise's.

It bothered him sometimes, generally during the couple of nights a week that they spent alone, that he was becoming so dependent on her for his happiness. That he couldn't imagine himself without Eloise. But since it was what she wanted too, he couldn't bring himself to voice his doubts about whether or not that was a bad thing.

She arrived at his flat late, after a Friday evening emergency at the hospital. Waiting for her smile made it all the more special, and she pulled a bundle of photographs from her handbag.

'I found yet another pile of photos. I really should organise them all and put them into albums. Or at least in the same place...'

Sam chuckled. Eloise printed her photographs out, and had a habit of using them as bookmarks and scattering them around in odd places, so that she came across them every now and then. His own photographs were carefully ordered and sorted, excluding those that provoked any kind of reaction, and he loved the way that she didn't feel the need to censor her childhood.

'I quite like seeing them in instalments. Particularly the ones you'd forgotten were even there.' Eloise had covered her face in embarrassment at a few of them.

'Ha! In that case, welcome to another episode of my horrible teenage fashion sense and mortifying attempts to seem sophisticated whenever someone whipped out a camera.'

'I love your teenage fashion sense. Would you like a glass of wine?' Sam had just poured himself one.

'A couple of sips of yours would be fine,

if you don't mind. I'm too tired for anything more.' She went into the sitting room, throwing herself down onto the sofa.

Sam joined her, pushing his glass across the coffee table towards her, and picking up the photographs. He knew most of the people in them now, her grandmother and her father, and older ones of her mother, which Eloise always paused over with a hint of regret.

'Is that Bess? And June?'

Eloise moved closer, looking over his shoulder. 'Yes, and the boy is Tom. She was going out with him for years, ever since they were sixteen.'

Another piece of her past that was as valuable to Sam as it was to Eloise. He flipped through the photographs, smiling at the ones of Paul engaged in renovating the old wall of the manor house.

And then... Eloise with a man he didn't know. She seemed different somehow, in a way that Sam couldn't quite put his finger on. Less animated, her smile less ebullient.

Eloise whipped the photograph from his hand. '*That* shouldn't be there...'

'Michael?' Sam asked before he could stop himself. If the photograph gave no hint of what Eloise might be thinking, her reaction now said it all.

She nodded, her cheeks reddening. The man was very handsome, and he and Eloise looked like the perfect couple. Jealousy stabbed at Sam, all the more virulent for being so unexpected.

'Hey! Don't do that.' He reached out, stopping her from tearing the photograph in two. He couldn't unsee the image now.

'It shouldn't be there, Sam. Michael's not a part of my life.'

Sam got her meaning, but she was making things worse. If Michael didn't mean something to her still, then she wouldn't need to pretend that he'd never existed. He took a breath, trying to steady the pounding of his heart. He should let this go, but he couldn't.

'Like it or not, he *was* a very big part of it. You can't just pretend that didn't happen, Eloise.'

Sam was trying to be calm. Trying to speak rationally, even though the fears and uncertainties that he'd dismissed as being part of his past were tearing at him. What if this relationship with Eloise really was too good to be true? If the process of finding their own space together meant that they were existing in a vacuum that couldn't withstand intrusions from the real world?

She was staring at the photograph, her

thoughts unreadable. The space between them seemed to be increasing with every moment that passed and, rather than let it just inexorably rip them apart, Sam got to his feet and walked over to the window.

'If you want me to tell you what happened with Michael, you should just say.' Eloise sounded hurt and Sam turned. There was still time to make this right.

'That's not what I mean, Eloise. Even if you never tell me…' He stopped to think for a moment. 'If you never tell me then it'll hurt, because I'll feel that there's still something that's wounded you and you can't trust me with it. But I can deal with that.'

She frowned. 'What *do* you want then?'

Good question. Sam didn't know. All he knew was that everything seemed to be suddenly out of control. He wanted to hold her and comfort her and calm all of her fears. But jealousy and anger were taunting him, telling him that he'd made a mistake in feeling that this could last, and all of his worst fears were justified.

'I want you to be free, Eloise. I don't know how you're going to do that. I don't have any suggestions. You'll have to work that out for yourself, because you won't tell me what happened.'

That came out much more angrily than he'd meant it to. Eloise heard it too, because she jutted her chin in a look of defiance.

So…what? What you said about my not needing to tell anyone because it was no one else's business…that was all just words, was it? What you thought you *should* say because it was what I wanted to hear?'

'That was then, Eloise. Are you telling me that nothing's happened between us since? That you still don't trust me?'

'No! Sam, I'm not going to do this with you. I'm not going to let you tell me how I should feel about something you know nothing about.'

'Tell me *why* I know nothing about it, why don't you?'

Raised voices. Angry words. Things said in the heat of the moment, that were the worst version of the truth. Sam didn't want this, and the only thing that he could do was turn his back on her, looking out of the window. For some reason, the world outside was just as it always had been, and hadn't burst into a fiery inferno.

They hadn't argued before. They'd disagreed, struggled to find common ground at times, and Sam had found that hard. But there had never been this unreasoning anger, which was distorting the balance of their relation-ship. He hadn't let that happen because he was afraid of it.

And now Sam knew why. He'd felt the force of his father's anger at times when he was a child, and seen what it had done to his mother. He'd made his own decision about the kind of man that he wanted to be and he didn't want to feel this senseless rage. Other people had arguments, got everything out of their system and then patched things up again. Not him. For Sam, every argument hacked away at his identity, casting him slowly adrift from the person that he wanted to be.

It was one of life's excruciating ironies that in encouraging him to express his own wants and needs Eloise had made him happy but also begun the process of splitting them apart. Sam could no longer pretend that he was able to function in a normal, healthy relationship.

'I should go.'

Had Eloise been reading his thoughts? Sam instantly began to regret them.

'What?'

He almost crumbled. Almost begged her to stay. And then he realised that Eloise under-stood exactly the same thing that he did. That neither of them could stop their past from in-terfering in their present, their future.

'I just want to go. Please.' Her voice trembled, but she knew what she was doing. And she was right to do it, even if it did hurt. Even if she knew that if she went now there was no coming back.

He turned, just in time to see her pressing her lips together, getting to her feet and storming out of the sitting room. He heard her pulling her coat out of the hall cupboard and the sound of her weekend bag being kicked across the floor. Then the front door slammed so hard that the glass skylight over the top of it rattled, and there was the sound of keys hitting the floor as she posted the copies he'd had made for her back through the letterbox.

Sudden nausea made him move, hurrying to the bathroom. He hadn't lost Eloise. He'd deliberately forced this separation. And, however much he wanted to, he knew that it would be wrong to ask her to stay.

And now…? As the shaking and the cold sweat began to subside, Sam made himself a promise. He could never let Eloise see him like this again. Angry. However much this hurt, he would let Eloise go.

CHAPTER THIRTEEN

SIX O'CLOCK IN the morning, and Eloise was on the train. Today was going to be a round trip of eleven hours—if she was lucky—and she wouldn't be home again until midnight. But it was necessary.

It had been a hard decision to leave Sam, but it was the right one. He'd been angry, but he'd been right—she wasn't done with the past any more than he was. After three weeks, she was still missing him as much as she had the moment she'd walked out on him. She'd cried and tried to sleep. Called a friend to get the name and number of a good counsellor, who'd listened to what she had to say and booked in another two-hour session later in the week. It was becoming increasingly obvious that there was still a lot to talk about.

She hadn't called Sam, and he hadn't called her. Eloise wondered whether he'd picked up the phone to do so as many times as she had.

But it wouldn't do any good. They both had too much baggage, too many unresolved issues. She'd left it a few days and then emailed Gramps to tell him that she and Sam were no longer together, in case he should be embarrassed by not knowing. Then she'd received an odd email from Celeste.

Eloise had written back, questioning it. Surely talking to Sam's mother wasn't really appropriate in the circumstances. She'd received an immediate reply, which read like the written equivalent of Celeste stamping her foot in exasperation.

Trust me. It's not mine to talk about, but I promise you that Elsa will welcome it.

Eloise had wondered whether there was anything that anyone could say that would make this right. But, even if it seemed hopeless, she couldn't let Sam go without taking this chance. Celeste and his mother would take care of him, the way that she couldn't any more, and maybe Sam's wounds would begin to heal. That would make all of this worthwhile.

Eloise had written a carefully worded email, and it had become obvious that Elsa's wish to speak to her was genuine and that there was something she wanted to say. This was far too important to do by email, or even a video call. France was a long way to go, but nowhere was too far if there was any hope of it helping Sam. So Eloise got onto a train, changing at Calais for the high-speed TGV service that went south, into the heart of France.

Elsa and her partner were standing together at the station, and Eloise recognised them from the photo they'd sent. It was left to Hugo, Elsa's partner, to keep the conversation going in the car. Elsa looked as nervous as Eloise was.

Elsa and Hugo's apartment was bright and beautifully decorated, with more than a trace of Sam's talent for interiors, only with a more feminine touch. Elsa led her into the sitting room, inviting her to sit down on a high-backed antique sofa.

'How long do you have, Eloise?'

'Three hours. We have plenty of time.' Maybe a few pleasantries first, to break the ice.

'Wonderful. Then you have time for lunch. I'll get busy…' Hugo smiled and left the two women alone.

Eloise fidgeted and smiled, and Elsa smiled back. 'How is Celeste?'

'Well, she and my grandfather seem extraordinarily happy together.'

'So I hear. Celeste saved my life, even though my ex-husband was her own brother. Her capacity for rolling up her sleeves and getting involved is…' Elsa's eyes glimmered with quiet humour '…wonderful. If a little startling at times.'

Eloise laughed, feeling instinctively drawn to Elsa's good-humoured kindness. 'Celeste's been very good to me too. And you're right, very surprising.'

'I owe her a great deal. I'll be going over to England in a week's time for a visit, and I'll be staying with Paul and Celeste for a few days. But I wanted to speak privately with you first.'

'I'm so pleased you've asked me. It's not something I'd expect, but I'm very grateful.'

'I think we've all seen the futility of taking sides. That silly business with the Douglases and the Grants has taught us all that. And there's something I want you to know about Sam.'

'You should know… I don't think there's any possibility that Sam and I will be getting back together again. There's just too much that we both have to get through.'

'I understand that. It may help you to know

how much Sam's had to face, and in truth it'll help me as well.'

'Then I'd like to thank you for wanting to share it with me.' The long train journey, and Elsa's wish to talk, already had Eloise on edge, but the atmosphere in the room was so full of things that were unsaid. It was enough to frighten the stoutest of hearts, and make the bravest of souls feel that retreat might be an option.

Stand your ground. If Sam never knows that you're brave enough to do this for him, then at least you will.

'You know that my divorce from Sam's father wasn't easy. He wouldn't accept it.' Elsa was looking at her steadily.

'Yes, Sam told me. He said that his father was…persistent.'

'Your word?' Elsa smiled. 'You don't need to be tactful with me, Eloise. I lived it, I know exactly what happened.'

'Sam said that his father was very angry. He came calling at all hours of the day and night, and wouldn't listen to you when you asked him to leave you alone.'

'That's true. One of the reasons I left Sam's father was that I didn't want my children to be affected by his anger. Sam was old enough to understand that, but maybe he saw that as a burden, rather than my wish to let him know that I'd always defend him.'

Elsa got to her feet, opening a drawer in the elegant sideboard and taking out a framed picture. Wordlessly, she handed it to Eloise.

For a moment she thought it was Sam. And then the style of the jeans and the woman sitting beside him told her that it wasn't. There was something different about the face too.

'This is…you? And Sam's father?'

Elsa nodded, clearly waiting for Eloise to come to her own conclusions. That wasn't so difficult and it was happening with stomach-turning speed.

'They're so alike. Apart from…'

'The nose.' Elsa smiled. 'That was Celeste's doing. Sam broke his nose at a rugby match and when Celeste set it for him she made him a little more handsome.'

Maybe Eloise should confess her own part in it all. That didn't matter right now. There were more important things to say. 'I've never seen a photograph of Sam's father. Although I suppose that his resemblance to Celeste should have made me realise he took after the Grants. I didn't think about it too much…'

But this was everything. The answer. When Sam looked in the mirror every day, he saw the man that he didn't want to be.

'Sam never really saw that his anger is so much more like Celeste's than his father's.'

Eloise thought for a moment. 'You mean... that impulse that Celeste has to go and do something about it, if she sees that something's wrong?'

'Yes, exactly. Sam has that same kind of passion, to make things better. Speaking as his mother, I believe that Sam could do anything he sets his mind to if he'd only allow himself to.'

'I think he could too. But he keeps that bottled up, because he doesn't want to be like his father.'

Elsa nodded. 'He needs someone like you, Eloise. Someone who cares about him enough to see that.'

'I need someone like him...' Eloise felt her eyes fill with tears.

'I won't make any suggestions about what you should do next. I just felt you should know.'

'Thank you. I really appreciate your talking with me. I know it can't have been easy.'

'A great deal easier than doing nothing.' Elsa took the photograph from Eloise's hands, as if it pained her to look at it too much, and put it back in the drawer. 'I'll go and see whether Hugo has a cup of tea for us. I have more photographs, of Sam when he was little. Would you like to see them?'

That was going to hurt. But Eloise had learned that sometimes hurt was necessary if you wanted to heal. 'I'd *love* to. Thank you.'

Sam had been driving himself hard. Running until he almost dropped from exhaustion, so that he'd get a night's sleep. Walking two extra miles for his patients, because the only way that he could squeeze any satisfaction out of his own life was to make a difference to theirs.

It wasn't working. In his dreams, he still heard the door slam, and then Eloise's keys falling to the floor as she posted them back through the letterbox. Still saw her face, and woke with a start to find she wasn't there.

He'd spent the weekend in Norfolk, after Aunt Celeste had called to invite him, obviously having caught wind of the fact that he and Eloise were no longer together. Aunt Celeste had made it clear that if he wanted to talk she would be pleased to listen, and he'd politely declined the offer, saying that it was over and he was pretty cut up about it, but there was nothing anyone could do.

He visited Joy Cornelius, who had just come out of rehab after her stroke, taking

French pastries and a packet of her favourite tea. Joy's quick arrival in hospital after her stroke had meant that she could be scanned, and that clot-busting drugs could be given, which had ameliorated the effects of the stroke considerably. Apart from a slight slur in her speech and a weakness in her hand, both of which were improving, Joy was her old self.

'It's so nice to see you, Sam. I never got to thank you properly for putting me in touch with the people at the Community Centre. They have some wonderful clubs and activities, and it's so nice to think that I can go there any time I get a little lonely.'

'All part of the service, Joy.'

'No, it's not. Eloise is lucky to have you, you're a kind man. I have her hat, by the way. I washed it for her to give it back. It was a lovely thought and very warm.'

Sam chuckled. 'I think she wanted you to have it.'

Joy beamed at him. 'Such a nice girl. You're lucky too.'

'Eloise and I are…' He didn't want to go into details about that. 'We're just friends.'

'Ah. So I've put my foot in my mouth, have I?'

'No, that's okay.' The thought that Joy's clear blue eyes had seen something between him and Eloise was making him feel oddly happy. Stripping away all of the complications and pain, and for one moment leaving him with just the connection that had brought the two of them together.

'We were together, but we decided to call it a day.' The words just slipped out, propelled by longing. As if the more people who knew, the more real it was.

'You let her get away?'

Sam picked up the rehab putty that he'd brought with him, moulding it into a ball. This was a little more firm than the one that Joy had been using, and she was ready for that now.

'Complicated.' He handed her the putty. 'Give this a try.'

Joy started to mould it with her fingers, nodding as she did so. 'It's a bit more difficult.'

'Yes, that's the idea.'

'Did you put up a fight?'

He supposed he deserved that. He'd just been giving Joy a friendly lecture about how she needed to push herself to regain full use of her hand.

'It's not my place to fight a woman.' He laughed as Joy raised her eyebrows. 'Only you, Joy, when you don't do your exercises.'

'That's not what I meant…' Joy gave him a knowing look, and tried again with the putty.

She didn't seem about to elaborate, and Sam should just leave it. Eloise wasn't coming back, and if she did he'd send her away again. But the one, small chance that Joy might have something to say, that could show Sam a way back to her, was nonetheless a chance. Which made it far too valuable to miss.

'What do you mean, then?'

Joy sighed. 'You're a clever man, Sam, but you don't know everything. You don't fight a woman to get her back. You fight *for* her.'

Sam nodded. 'I see. Thanks…' Suddenly the world had opened up. Sam had no clue what fighting *for* Eloise meant in practical terms, but this was one of those times when one little word made all the difference.

He smiled at Joy, picking up the booklet that lay beside her on the coffee table. 'Shall we have a look at the exercises your physiotherapist left you? Just go through them again and make sure that you're doing them correctly…'

CHAPTER FOURTEEN

TRY AS HE MIGHT, Sam couldn't get the words out of his head. Fighting Eloise, imposing his own will on her, was a shameful thing to do, and he'd avoid that at all costs. Fighting *for* her seemed a lot more honourable.

Of course there was a practical side to it all. What he wanted was to have Eloise back. That was obvious. How to fight for her? That was a little less clear.

He wondered whether he should call Alice. Apologise and ask her out for coffee, to see if she'd give him any insights about why she'd left. And what could have stopped her. And then Sam realised. He didn't need closure, not any more. He didn't need anyone else to tell him who he was, because all he needed to be was the man who loved Eloise. Now, his only decision was *when* to do what he knew he must.

Even that was taken from him when he

found himself getting up early on Saturday morning, deciding not to give shaving a miss and selecting a sweater that matched his shirt instead of just grabbing whatever was clean. By the time he got to his car it was as if there had never been any choice in the matter.

All the same, he faltered before walking up Eloise's front path. The curtains in the sitting room were closed, and he wondered whether he'd come too early. Then he saw her at the window, drawing the curtains back. His heart almost stopped as she darted backwards and then the front door swung open.

'Sam… Sam, please don't go.' She looked so beautiful. Hair wet from the shower still, and a loose yellow sweater with jeans. Like all of the Saturday mornings he could ever want, rolled into one.

'I'm not coming in.' He walked up the front path, stopping in the porch.

'Why not?' Eloise frowned at him.

'I want to ask you…if you'll come to my place some time… To talk. I could cook dinner.'

'What's going on? Why can't you come in and talk now, since you're here?'

That was an alteration to the plan that he hadn't anticipated. 'I've made my mind up and I don't want to give up on what we had together. I thought that an invitation would give you time to think about how you felt about that.'

'Sam.' She gave him the smile that had always let him know that things were all right. 'If you think I'm going to endure your cooking, just for the convenience of having time to think, then I don't need it. I have something I have to say to you and I was going to give you a call today and ask you over.'

She led the way into the sitting room. He noticed that the easy chairs were still where he'd suggested she place them, pushed back a little into the bay window to give the room a little more space. The large coffee table in front of the sofa still had the shimmering glass bowl that he'd found in the kitchen at its centre. Eloise had great taste, but she thought she didn't and tended not think too much about making the most of her rooms by arranging them nicely.

None of that mattered. It was just easier to think about that than what he'd come here to do. Because now that he *was* here, it was difficult to imagine what he could possibly say that would persuade Eloise to take him back.

All Eloise wanted to do was fling herself into Sam's arms. That would be the easy way to go, because they could rely on the connection between them to smooth over everything else. The harder, stonier path was through all of the things that were keeping them apart, and that was the one that they had to take if they were going to work anything out between them.

She sat down on the sofa. Sam retreated to the other side of the room, sitting in one of the easy chairs in the window.

'Sam, your mother contacted me.' That wasn't quite right, and she had to choose her words better than this. 'Actually, Celeste did and said that your mother wanted to talk to me, and I contacted her…'

He smiled. 'I get the picture. Mum and Celeste executed a pincer movement. They do that kind of thing.'

At least he didn't seem too upset by it. That had been the first of Eloise's concerns. 'So I went to France…'

His eyebrows shot up. 'You went all that way? For a chat?'

'I thought it was important, and it turned out that it was. I would have gone a lot further than that, because she was very kind to me and…she helped me see some things more clearly.'

'I'm grateful to you for making the journey.' Sam looked at her thoughtfully. 'I think you'd better tell me what she had to say.'

'She showed me something. A picture of your father.' She saw the shock in Sam's eyes, but he said nothing. 'It must have been so hard for you, knowing how much you looked like him and wanting to be different.'

Sam nodded, rubbing his nose thoughtfully. 'You really did do me a favour when you kidnapped the Douglas team's star rugby player.'

It was so like Sam to try to turn the conversation to a lighter note. But Eloise wasn't going to allow him to distract her.

'Celeste made a good job of it, so I won't disagree with you there. That's not the point. What I want to say to you is that we all inherit a few things from our parents. The way they bring us up puts a few more things into the mix. But, ultimately, I believe we have free will. You are the man you've chosen to be.'

'It's a nice thought…'

'No, it's not just a nice thought. I can see why you would think differently. Your mother told me that one of the reasons she left your father was that she wanted a better life for you and your brother and sister—'

'That's a nice way of saying that she saw his anger in me, isn't it?' Sam turned the corners of his mouth down.

'No, it isn't. She told me that if you were like any of the Douglases you were like Celeste. I agreed with her. Celeste doesn't take any nonsense from anyone, but she uses her passion to make things better.'

Eloise was beginning to feel breathless, fear tearing at her. Sam's reaction seemed resigned, as if this was something that couldn't be changed and would always haunt him. She was fighting for them, and she needed him to as well.

He was here, though. Eloise had spent five days thinking about this and still hadn't managed to work up the courage to get into her car and go and ring his doorbell.

'The reason I didn't get married was...'

Sam held his hand up. 'I don't need to know.'

'I need to tell you. You were right. I haven't let go of Michael properly, and that's not fair on you. You deserve to be trusted.' Eloise took a breath, trying to steady herself. 'The day before we were due to get married, I was sorting through some papers, trying to find Michael's passport, and I found some other papers, pertaining to unpaid maintenance for a child. I asked him what they were, and he told me that he'd been in a relationship before he met me.'

Sam nodded. 'That happens.'

'Yes, but what doesn't happen is that you leave someone when they're pregnant, and then pretend they don't exist when you make a new relationship. He hadn't even seen his child, and even though there was a maintenance order in place he'd stopped paying. It wasn't just the lies. How could I marry a man who was willing to turn his back on his own child?'

'And you didn't tell anyone? Why not?'

'I thought everyone knew that we'd cancelled the wedding. We wrote an email together, and he started to get really angry. *"Get out of my sight"* were his exact words. Then the next day he turned up at the church, with everyone there, and pretended he'd been stood up at the altar. I didn't know that he hadn't sent the email until I got back, and by that time… Michael could be very charming and he'd persuaded everyone that I'd just run out on him.'

She could feel tears running down her cheeks. 'That was why I left you. Because I wasn't ready to tell you the truth. I was afraid to tell you what really happened, that you wouldn't be on my side. I couldn't bear to hear you telling me to get out of your sight.'

She couldn't even look at Sam, let alone meet his gaze.

'It hurt. But that's on me, because I wouldn't take the risk of trying to stop you. I've thought about this, and I'm not afraid of telling you that I want to be with you.'

He got to his feet, coming to sit down on the sofa next to her. Sam took her hands in his and Eloise clung on tight.

'But what do we do now, Sam? Can we even get over all of the things that have happened to us?' Eloise's courage failed her for a moment.

But he was there for her. Sam tipped her chin up, catching her gaze. 'We stop fighting each other, and we fight *for* each other. When I falter you hold me up. And when you falter I'll take you in my arms and carry you.'

'Sam… Don't say that unless you really mean it…' She didn't dare believe him, because she wanted to so much.

'I mean it. If you kiss me now, I'll never run from you again, and I won't let you run either, however hard it gets. Don't imagine that's necessarily a good thing, because we have a lot to work through and it may get very hard.'

'Bring it on, Sam.'

He kissed her. Not the tenderness of a reconciliation, but the raw possessiveness of a man who knew what he wanted and was going to fight for it.

'I want you to marry me. You can say yes or you can say no. It won't make any difference...'

Eloise grinned at him. No one but Sam could make a proposal quite like that and make it sound as if he was offering her everything that she'd ever wanted.

'You mean you don't mind which? No is as good as yes?'

He shot her a reproachful look. 'I mean that I'll love you whatever you say. I'll want to be with you and fight for our relationship. You might feel it's a little too hard...' He was teasing her back now.

'The harder the better. Yes.'

He laughed out loud, an expression of relieved joy. 'Yes. Really?'

'Yes, Sam. Are you worried I won't turn up?'

'No, because I'm not going to let you go.'

She could hear his heartbeat as he held her close. Honest and true, the heart that she would always cherish.

'We'll be busy for the next couple of days, then.' He smiled, kissing her cheek.

'Busy? Why, what are we going to do?'

'My mother and Hugo are up in Norfolk at the moment, with Paul and Aunt Celeste. They'll all be down in London on Wednesday, and by then I'll have to have bought you an engagement ring, and taken you to a romantic proposal dinner.'

'But you've just proposed. If you think this was just a trial run you can forget it, Sam, because I've said yes now, and I'm holding you to it.'

'Good. I'm holding you to it as well. Only Mum and Aunt Celeste are going to want to see the ring and hear all about my efforts in making the perfect romantic evening to propose to you. And Paul's definitely going to want to know that I'm a suitable husband-to-be, who'll treat you as you deserve to be treated. So I figured we might do it all over again before Wednesday. If you don't mind, that is.'

She hugged him tight. Sam knew how important family was to her, and sharing this with them was perfect. 'I think it's a beautiful idea. Aren't you forgetting something, though?'

'I'm not forgetting anything. This afternoon will be quite soon enough to go and choose a ring, because I'm rather hoping that this morning you'll be otherwise occupied.'

The come-to-bed look in his eyes told her just what he had in mind.

'I was rather hoping I might be too…'

CHAPTER FIFTEEN

Six months later

THE MAN SHE'D met had been paralysed by self-doubt. And the man Eloise had married today was free to love her with his whole heart.

Sam had freed her as well. There had been arguments, silences and fears that had to be spoken about before they could be dismissed. But through it all they'd loved one another. Eloise had never felt such happiness, and she knew that Sam felt the same way.

Their wedding had been held in the tiny church near to Gramps and Celeste's Norfolk home. Eloise had set her heart on a winter wedding, after they'd settled in to their new house, but their plans had suddenly changed. When she'd walked downstairs five weeks ago, clutching the pregnancy test, Sam had hugged her tightly then fallen to his knees, begging her to marry him now, because he couldn't wait another moment.

Five weeks wasn't long to plan a wedding, but it had been done with such joy that everything had just fallen into place. The reception was held in the garden of the manor house, and as darkness fell the guests had begun to leave and the caterers started to clear up. Gramps had fetched lanterns from the house, hanging them in the pagoda on the lawn, and Sam and Eloise joined him and Celeste there, together with Elsa and Hugo.

'This is so pretty. Do you think we can get something like it for our wedding, Paul?' Celeste asked.

'I could build one.' Gramps liked nothing better than a construction project. 'Style it in keeping with the house, with maybe a fire pit and some kind of removable glazing for the winter.'

Celeste caught her breath. 'That would be lovely! With roses around the perimeter...'

'We've done it now.' Sam leaned over to kiss Eloise. 'There's no stopping them, is there?'

'There's no stopping us either.'

She'd loved every moment of the last six months. Sam had loved her so well, so faithfully, that even the arguments, the moments when one or the other of them had faltered momentarily, had been an expression of how they were moving forward together.

All she had to do was touch his hand, to see him smile and feel the warmth of his gaze. Sam was sure of her love as well, and they could look forward to the future.

'When Celeste caught Eloise's bouquet by mistake...' Gramps was recounting the highlights of the day now '...and shouted, *"Eloise, you missed!"* and threw it again.'

Elsa was laughing too. 'I caught sight of it coming straight at me and ducked. Hugo had to catch it for me.'

'Taking aim with a bunch of flowers isn't as easy as it looks. But it got to the right place in the end.' Eloise grinned at Elsa. 'So have you and Hugo decided where you're going to get married yet?'

'We thought London. We'll be moving back when Hugo's current work contract expires, and our families are here. Perhaps I can come and stay with you, in your lovely new house, to scout out a few locations?'

Sam chuckled. 'Whenever you want, Mum. Although it's a lovely undecorated house at the moment.'

'That's why we need Elsa.' Eloise nudged

him. 'She'll be able to give me some ideas for the nursery.'

Sam smiled, leaning forward to kiss her. 'You *know* I can't wait to get started with that. Another six months is a long time to wait.'

'It'll go so fast.' Elsa laughed. 'Before you know it, they'll be packing their bags and going to medical school.'

'Or…anywhere else they want to go,' Sam added.

'That sounds like a fine idea to me. Far too many doctors in the family already. We need a few…' Celeste paused, obviously trying to think of another job that might appeal, and everyone laughed.

'I'm going to propose a toast.' Paul rose, catching up the last champagne bottle from the ice bucket and adding a drop to everyone's glasses, while Sam fetched sparkling water for Eloise.

'Aloysius Grant and Henry Douglas had no idea what their falling-out might lead to. Celeste and I fell in love while in vigorous confrontation over some minor detail concerning Grant College and Douglas College.'

Celeste laughed. 'Until someone reported us for holding hands in the quad, and we were each thrown off our respective committees for conflict of interest.'

'Then Sam and Eloise had the great good luck, although no one quite knew it at the time, to be the only guests at our engagement party. And now we're looking forward to Baby Grant-Douglas, who will be a much-loved addition to our new blended family of Douglas and Grant.'

Eloise felt Sam squeeze her hand. He was so excited about becoming a father. Their baby would grow up at the heart of a close and loving family.

'And now, on the very day that Eloise and Sam are married, our beloved Elsa accepted Hugo's proposal.'

'Elsa turned me down six times, but seven is my lucky number.' Hugo laughed, kissing Elsa's hand.

'So, ladies and gentlemen, please raise your glasses to Henry Douglas and Aloysius Grant. Misguided they may have been, but they have brought us all much happiness, laughter and love.'

'Now and for ever.' Sam whispered the words as he and Eloise joined in with the toast.

'Douglas and Grant!'

* * * * *